bush oranges

kay donovan

Penguin Books

Penguin Books

Penguin Group (Australia)
250 Camberwell Road, Camberwell, Victoria 3124, Australia
Penguin Books Ltd
80 Strand, London WC2R 0RL, England
Penguin Group (USA) Inc.
375 Hudson Street, New York, New York 10014, USA
Penguin Books, a division of Pearson Canada
10 Alcorn Avenue, Toronto, Ontario, Canada M4V 3B2
Penguin Group (NZ)
cnr Airborne and Rosedale Roads, Albany, Auckland 1310, New Zealand
Penguin Books (South Africa) (Pty) Ltd
24 Sturdee Avenue, Rosebank, Johannesburg 2196, South Africa
Penguin Books India (P) Ltd
11, Community Centre, Panchsheel Park, New Delhi 110 017, India

First published by Penguin Books Australia Ltd, 2001
This paperback edition published by Penguin Group (Australia), a division of
Pearson Australia Group Pty Ltd, 2004

1 3 5 7 9 10 8 6 4 2

Cover design by Louise Leffler © Penguin Group (Australia)
Text design by Melissa Fraser © Penguin Group (Australia)
Cover illustration by Rosanna Vecchio
Typeset in 10/15.5 Stempel Schneidler by Post Pre-Press Group, Brisbane, Queensland
Printed and bound in Australia by McPherson's Printing Group, Maryborough,
Victoria

National Library of Australia
Cataloguing-in-Publication data:

Donovan, Kay.
Bush oranges.
ISBN 0 14 100641 2.
A823.3

This project has been assisted by the Commonwealth Government through the
Australia Council, its arts funding and advisory body.

To my mother
in memory of Eunice

THE MINTON FAMILY

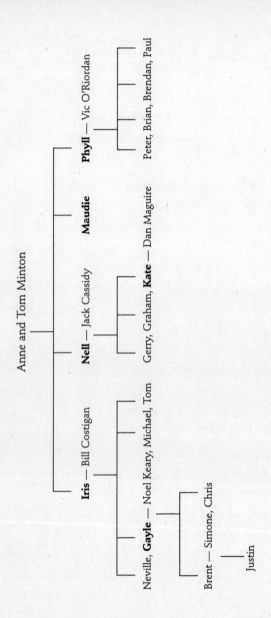

Anne and Tom Minton

Iris — Bill Costigan

Nell — Jack Cassidy

Maudie

Phyll — Vic O'Riordan

Neville, **Gayle** — Noel Keary, Michael, Tom

Gerry, Graham, **Kate** — Dan Maguire

Peter, Brian, Brendan, Paul

Brent — Simone, Chris

Justin

KATE

You can sense when a cyclone is brewing.

Small, seemingly insignificant changes filter into your perception, creeping in through the half-open back door of your consciousness and confounding your awareness with the presence or absence of those things which, in the usual course of a day, slip past you unobserved. Things like the texture of the air, the shape of a reflection, the stillness and the quiet. Especially the quiet.

There is a difference between the normal quiet of a tropical day and the complete stillness that precedes a cyclone. The birds sense it early and leave. Every breath of wind stops so that even the small movement of a breeze through leaves is stilled. If you have never experienced a cyclone before, you will be unaware of all these things, but, after the first time, you always remember the signs. It's a brooding kind of quiet, a sense of something impending, a warning to make urgent preparations: to fill the bathtub with water and nail down any loose sheets of corrugated iron. The blanket of heat that normally settles over the middle of a tropical day can't silence the chorale of small sounds that fill your ears. The air resounds with the buzzing of a million tiny movements, from the vibration of a leaf in hot sunlight to the little shake of a twig, as an otherwise imperceptible breeze fills the background. Then it stops . . . Dead quiet. It seems as if in one moment the sound and all the movement are sucked out, leaving only the vacuum that precedes the cyclone. These observations sit at the edge of your consciousness ready to fill you with information, if only you can read the signs.

My childhood was punctuated by cyclones that threatened us, stalking ominously up and down the coast or raging in from the sea only to twist away at the last minute, menacing the townships with their capriciousness. I was nearly an adult before I experienced the full force of my first cyclone and since then there have been many more.

First comes the wind. Short fierce gusts rattle the roof and tear at the trees. Then rain, sharp needles of water thrown at the ground. The sky shrouds the earth so there's no way out. It's a storm, you think. It will soon pass. But it isn't and it doesn't and the wind builds to a gale. Angry at being ignored, it whips the world into a frenzy of whirling and blasting and ripping at everything in its way.

My Nana, Annie Minton, once told me the story about the great cyclone Leonta, which hit the town when she was still just a girl. It was the first recorded cyclone in the young settlement's history and it shocked the township with its force. Houses were left in splinters. Trees and crops were stripped of every leaf, and buildings were blown apart. Out in the channel the steamship *Lucinda* went down as she struggled toward the harbour. Inside the house where Annie lived with her sisters and parents, the family listened fearfully to the creaking of the walls. With every gust the house shuddered as if the wind would shake it apart. Annie's father stood guard at the wooden shutters on the side of the house away from the onslaught of the wind. At the height of the storm he ordered Annie to take his place so he could fix the sheet of tin that the wind threatened to tear away from the lean-to kitchen.

That's when she saw it.

Standing at the shutters, looking down a hill now stripped of vegetation by the force of the storm, she saw what looked like a huge snake twisting and curling its way up from one of the warehouses by the harbour. It shone white against the dark clouds as it wound up and around in seamless movements across the bruised sky.

She imagined it was one of those cane-and-paper kites the Chinese brought out on celebration days. Just as quickly, reason told her there was no way such a flimsy construction could fly so elegantly in the maelstrom now sweeping around them. It was like some spirit of the wind, a huge white worm that lived in the wild heart of the cyclone and could only enjoy its release when the storm was at its peak.

She called her sister, Maggie, and the two of them

peered through the shutters so intently that they drew the others. 'What can it be?' they exclaimed, their attention so focused on that strange flying object, wildly curling and unfurling on the wind, that they were distracted from the damage being wreaked around them. That's how their father found them when he came back into the room, soaked and windblown from his efforts to secure the tin. 'Why, 'tis plates,' he said, 'enamel plates from Burns Philp storehouse. They only come in on yesterday's delivery. Tomorrow, there be free plates for miles by t' look of it.'

I have often sat at the Point and looked out over the channel that separates us from the mainland, taking in the sailing boats, the range of mountains in the distance and the changes the weather writes on the surface of the water. Often I think about Annie's parents as they sailed along the coastline and dropped anchor at the head of the river. I wonder what crossed their minds as they stood on deck on their last evening aboard and studied the mangroves lining the shore and the impressive rock silhouetted against a fading orange sunset. I wonder if they thought about their children's children and about their descendants, and whether they would still be here a hundred years on. More likely their minds were full of the immediate concerns of finding a home and food and work.

It's the fate of some families to be dispersed by the elements. Every couple of generations, some act of God picks them up and throws them haphazardly around the world.

When Annie's parents gathered their scanty possessions and walked away from the Famine, they went in search of a better life on this side of the globe. I like to think they chose the great adventure they embarked on. It is more stirring than to have them just run away from the harsh hand that fate had dealt them back there. And what a world they saw on their way here, those two Irish peasants, weary of starvation and the daily menacing of English overlords. They spent two months on board ship with porpoises and flying fish as their occasional travelling companions. For their curious daughters, born safe in the new land and eager to hear tales of excitement, they would recount the dangers of high seas in the Bay of Biscay, the strangeness of the orange-sellers at Port Said, the bizarre snake-charmers and scantily clad natives of the Spice Islands. Their stories filled the nights after dinner and the minds of their three young girls, who grew rosy and strong and grateful that their parents had come to Arcadia, this new land that drew honest workers in search of a better life. Its roughness deterred the genteel English who favoured the colonies in India and the Indies, where they strove to replicate the lives they wished they could have had back home, and where servants were more easily come by. North Queensland was a place for people prepared to earn their rewards. For men of vision there were rich farming lands on the coastal plain and tin, iron and cattle. For men of dreams, like Annie's father, there was gold, and, while he had his health, there was only gold.

Now barely a handful of their descendants live here. Even I live elsewhere and it is only the strings of family and memory that still tie me to this place. Scattered lives are like leaves, sprouted from the same tree in the same corner of bush, torn apart and flung about by the winds before coming to land, perhaps in some shaded gully or on some exposed and barren rock, all of them to crumble or rot in the end.

The sideboard in my mother's dining room is full of souvenirs from all over the world, reminders of holidays with her children in their temporary homes in cities she never dreamed she would visit. Gerry and Graham both live overseas and I, her youngest child by many, many years and her only daughter, have made a life of my own down south. I come back from time to time for holidays, but prodigal daughters are not received in the same way as prodigal sons.

Auntie Iris lives in a sparse room in a nursing home. A sign outside her door embellishes her name, Iris Costigan, with the flowers and ribbons of folk art and marks her ownership of this small space. Inside, there is nowhere to display a lifetime's collection of trinkets and ornaments. There's not even room for the Victorian easychair that was hers from Nana's house. The bare brick walls are covered with framed photos of her children – her daughter Gayle, her sons and their wives, their children and Gayle's precious new grandson. 'Here's Neville and Christine,' she tells her visitors, or the staff, or anyone who'll stop for a moment to listen. 'Here they are in front of the . . . What's it called? That Italian tower. In Pizza . . . yes, that's it. That's on their honeymoon, and here they are with the new baby on holiday last summer. They went to some island near Malta. They're moving to New York next month. Michael and Bev and the children are getting together with them for Christmas.' Her voice grows thin and drops to a whisper as she grabs an arm and says, 'Thank the Lord Gayle's lot stayed around or I'd be a lonely old lady like Nell.'

Maudie Minton lives in a haze of dementia, propped up on pillows in the same nursing home in a suburb that was once an outer suburb of town. Now it's barely half an hour's ride from the city centre. Its neatly planted gardens have huge shade trees and thick bushes and the children from the nearby housing estate have grown up and moved further out to suburbs that are filled with the playful cries of their children. Maudie doesn't know that those suburbs exist. She doesn't even know her sisters any more.

In her dining room Auntie Phyll has a dresser, a sleek sixties piece of chrome, glass and veneer where postcards from her children sit amongst fishing trophies and framed photos of Uncle Vic's prize catches. Each year there's a new row of postcards lining the shelves. None of the old ones are ever thrown away. The rows just grow deeper and deeper.

My mother and her sisters still live in this town where they were born, grew up, made friends, went to church, married and raised families – or didn't. They are old. They have friends and memories and familiar surroundings but not family. The next generation has long gone to live in places as far apart as any cyclone could scatter them.

From the day I got my first period, my mother prayed I would not fall pregnant. I swear she prayed so hard God fused my tubes. Mum never taught me the facts of life but she did subject me to regular talks on chastity and the importance of a girl keeping her virtue. Of course, she never once mentioned sex. She relied mostly on oblique references to 'staying pure' and 'keeping yourself for marriage', but I knew what her real concern was. She let it slip one night across the washing up, after telling me a cautionary tale of a desperate girl who had 'lost her chastity'. Her voice fell to an undertone as she muttered, 'We don't want no bastard children in this family.'

It has been a long, tiresome day. Since February, when Dan and I started the in-vitro program, my cycle and a team of fertility experts have ruled our lives. The hormone injections send my moods from one extreme to another and I can never tell whether I'm going to lash out or cry. I lie on the floor staring up through the windows at the empty blue sky and try to let the day slide away.

The ringing is loud and insistent and I can't find the phone. Dan has a habit of leaving the handset lying where he last used it. I hate living in chaos and I hate leaving the telephone unanswered. People hang up when they hear the answering machine and I would rather take yet another market survey than be left wondering who called.

I expect it to be Dan to say he is on his way home. It seems as if his office hours get longer and longer until I think he might as well sleep there. I used to think living together would be cosy, sharing suppers and cuddling up in front of the telly. More and more it seems as if we need to make appointments just to have a meal together. I don't know how we ever talked for long enough to agree to have a child.

The handpiece is under the remains of last weekend's papers which are still spread over the coffee table and the sofa. By the time I find it my voice sounds anxious.

'Are you all right?' says my mother on the other end of the line.

'Of course I am,' I answer sharply and immediately bite my tongue. 'I couldn't find the phone.'

'Have I rung too late?' she says. 'I get the times mixed up with daylight saving.'

'That's okay.'

It is only eight o'clock for her but nine for me. There are cheap rates after eight and the distance between us is enough to make any reasonable person conscious of the cost of a long distance call.

Mum used to write letters, careful letters. She would write out a draft, then painstakingly edit it for anything that the reader could possibly misinterpret before she copied it out afresh in the neat flowing lines of her script. She is a careful woman, anxious not to give offence. She treats people's feelings like the precious objects she used to wrap and store well out of reach until my curious childish fingers could handle them safely.

She hesitates at her end of the line and I know she is working out how to phrase her next comment. She picks and chooses her words so carefully it's no wonder I accuse her of deviousness and manipulation. Just give it to me straight, I want to say. Snap, snap!

'It's Maudie, I'm afraid.' She pauses, leaving time for me to speak, for an intake of breath that doesn't come. 'Another stroke,' she says and pauses again. She waits for me to reach into the space with my questions and save her from having to volunteer all the details.

The call leaves me with a vague feeling – prescience, but of what I can't locate. The hairs rise on my lower back and my upper arms constrict as if two hands have grabbed me and are holding me in place. The shiver that started in my belly spreads upwards and leaves me shaking. Maudie. My mad, crazy aunt, Maudie, who's always lived on the border of childish and childlike. She is like an invisible friend you grow up with and then leave behind. I always feared I would wake one day and find that I had grown into Maudie. My worst nightmare was the one where I would suddenly realise life had passed me by and I could never embrace it, never feel the passion that makes the rest of it, the mundane everydayness of it, worthwhile.

That was the fear that drove me here, to the city, to this apartment and eventually to Dan. Get out. Get away. Get a life. Don't be a Maudie, a person who seemed to exist only as company for her mother, single and wasted. Instead I have a career and a home and a partner. I have a social circle, a wardrobe of business suits, a hair stylist and a gym membership. Mum thinks I live extravagantly. I don't care so long as I live.

I stayed with Nana and Maudie once, just for a few weeks when I was fourteen. Dad used his long-service leave to take Mum on a holiday. They called it their second honeymoon. Gerry and Graham were grown up, so they could look after themselves and I went to Nana and Maudie's. There wasn't a spare bedroom for me so Nana screened off one end of the living room and they moved in my bed and desk from home. I got my period three days after Mum and Dad left.

I've always had really painful periods but they were worse in the first few years. I lay in my bed, clutching a hot-water bottle to my abdomen, waiting for its warmth to soothe me through the aspirin. Maudie arrived back from work, opening the door with a loud bang in her usual fashion and shouting, 'I'm home. Where are you all?' Nana replied in whispered tones but Maudie was always slow to catch on. 'Sick? What's wrong with her?'

Her bags thumped on the floor at the end of my bed and her voice boomed into the corner. 'Are you dragging the chain in there?' she said, and gave the metal bedstead a good shake. Nana's voice broke in sharp and agitated: 'Come away at once, Maud, and leave Kate in peace.' The quick shuffling of her house slippers and the trail of creaking sounds told me that she had grabbed Maudie and propelled her across the linoleum. Nana's furious whispers and Maudie's stuttered replies filtered on the breeze through the curtained doorway. The house went silent and I dozed.

I felt the movement as Maudie sat on the bed. She leant across and brushed my forehead and the smell of sweat from her walk home in the afternoon sun still hung heavily around her. I rolled away and closed my eyes. Maudie patted the back of my head. This was not the bullying playmate I was used to and her attentiveness made me uncomfortable. I almost preferred the rough handling she had given me earlier, but mostly I resented her intrusion, planting herself on my bed uninvited. Please God, prove you exist. Don't let her start asking questions! I remembered overhearing Dad say that Maudie would kill you with kindness if you were sick but she'd let you drop dead in the street if she thought you were well. If I hadn't felt so bad, I would have got up and danced on the table to escape her solicitations. When she finally spoke it was in strange, hushed tones. 'You never want to get married, Katey love. It's better not to have anything to do with men.'

NELL

The ferry's late.

Of all the mornings for it to happen, it has to be this one. Phyll and Vic will be hanging about for me at the other end and there's no way I can get in touch, not that it would do any good. It wouldn't get me there any quicker. I don't like causing inconvenience, especially when Vic goes out of his way to do me a favour, but there's no point stewing over something I can't control.

I don't wait out on the jetty these days. My legs are a bit shaky and it can get very blowy out there. I stay up here on the esplanade until the boat rounds the reef to come up to the landing. That's when I wander down. There's no need to rush. They pull in to the jetty and the passengers get off while the deckhands unload and load the goods. They can see me coming and Brian, my neighbour, often catches the same ferry. He generally tells them I'm on my way, if he doesn't walk down with me himself. The locals here, they keep an eye out for me.

I knew the ferry was going to be late. When I got here, it was only just coming out of the breakwater. You can see it even though it's no more than a white speck in the distance and I can pick it easily. After all, I've been watching for it for sixty-odd years. Once it's clear of the harbour, it takes another twenty-five minutes to cross the channel. The ferries have been making the trip since I was a girl, so they ought to have the timing down pat by now. Not this boat, of course. This one's the big catamaran they brought into service ten years ago. Before that they had the old wooden boats.

The *Manderlay* was the biggest of them. It had a downstairs cabin where the men gathered to play cards when the yacht squadron held its moonlight cruises around the Island. It was always smoky down there and crowded up on the main deck, too crowded for dancing. Vic Foley's Orchestra played all the latest dance tunes and we'd gather around with our song sheets and join in one song after another. There were some hearty singers, especially among the men. I wasn't the musical type so it usually took some persuasion from Iris to get me to join in, but there was one night when I was in high spirits. My cheeks were flushed and my balance was a little unsteady, despite the calmness of the sea. I was floating in a cloud of Lily of the Valley that Jack had given me for my birthday a few weeks before. I knew he was going to pop the question. Iris and I agreed that the moonlight cruise was a likely time. When he and Bill climbed up from the card den, Iris and I were pouring soft drinks. Jack suggested we go up to the front deck where it was cooler, but Iris discreetly drew Bill away and left us to ourselves.

The bay was smooth as silk and the moon threw a long trail right across the water. We sat on the bench up in the prow and listened to the slap as it hit the ocean. Behind us the reverberations of the motor underscored the band as it struck up 'Let The Rest Of The World Go By', and right at that moment I knew what Jack was going to do. He lit a cigarette and looked back over my shoulder toward the Island, then he asked me. I couldn't speak. I clasped my hands in my lap and grinned like some silly buffoon. Mrs Jack Cassidy was exactly who I wanted to be. Finally he took my hand and said, 'So is that a yes?' and all I could do was nod.

I've still got that scent bottle tucked in amongst my hankies at home. And I've still got the dance cards, theatre programs, invitations . . . 'The Young Spinsters of the St Francis Parish invite Miss Ellen (Nell) Minton to a Grand Euchre Party and Dance, School of Arts, Thursday, 1st May 1939, Tickets 2/–.' I've saved them all.

Over here on the Island they think of me as Old Mrs Cassidy, though they're too polite to say it to my face. My daughter Kate, she laughs at that. She pretends to be them talking behind my back, saying things like 'Oh that Old Mrs Cassidy. She's good for her age, you know. Still goes to town once a week. You'd never believe she was eighty-three, the way she gets about.' Kate's always geeing me along even when I don't feel like it any more.

Phyllis and Vic are always on at me to move back to town and into the Home. What would I be wanting to do that for? I have my own home. My neighbours are good to me. I can manage my own meals and washing. And I like the doctor here. She has a nice manner and she listens to me. 'No way,' I say. 'I'm staying put till I go under.'

Jack and I came over here when the boys were young. We got the house as a holiday place when it was just a rough hut that the lifesavers had put up so they would have some shelter while they built their clubhouse. Jack made them an offer and got it at a good price. He didn't tell me he was buying it. He came home and said, 'How would you like to go to the Island for the weekend?' Then he spun me a story about getting the rental cheaply from a fellow at work who had to cancel his plans at the last moment. We packed in two minutes flat and just made it to the ferry, trailing children and bags. What a sight we must have been!

When we got to the Island, there was hardly enough light for us to pick our way along the track that straggled through the grass and gum trees up to the house. The trees were alive with the noise of birds coming in to nest, and I could hear the mournful cries of a colony of curlews from the bush at the back of the house. Jack drew the key from his pocket and slid it into the lock. Then he threw the door open and turned to me. 'Mrs Cassidy,' he said, 'welcome to your Island estate.' Well, I felt like I had just won the Golden Casket, and that night the boys and Jack and I gathered around, with only our bags to sit on, and ate a feast of tinned sardines on bread in the light of the hurricane lamp.

Off and on we talked about moving over permanently but the time never seemed right. You couldn't then, not with a young family and all. There wasn't electricity in those days, or running water. We had to make do with tank water and you learnt very quickly to use that sparingly. The toilet was a thunderbox right up the back of the yard and the nightsoil man came once a week to empty it. Things have changed a lot over here since then. They've got the primary school for the little ones now but the older ones still have to go to town. How their parents manage with all the ferry tickets, I don't know. Some families have two or three children going off to school each day and the father having to get to work. Even with the student concessions they must pay a pretty penny for the fares.

Jack and I didn't have the income they get today, but our money seemed to go further and the children never went without. We enjoyed ourselves but then I suppose our pleasures were simple ones. We did more things together. Nowadays people rely too much on organised entertainment. We used to make our own fun. My daughter would give me curry if she could hear me say that. 'Listen to you talk,' she'd say. 'Every time I ring you're never there. Always off having a good time, gadding about the neighbourhood, spending your money.' Oh well, at my time of life what's the use of having it if you can't enjoy it?

I only go to town once a week now unless there's something special to take me there. Like today. When Phyll rang last night, there was no question of not going. 'Vic and I will pick you up in town like regular.' They've been very good to me. If I ever want taking anywhere, it's just a matter of asking. All I've got to worry about is getting myself onto the boat at this end. Mind you, I'm very careful not to take advantage and every so often I buy Vic a Casket ticket. You never know. We might win the big one, one day.

I knew straight away that it was to do with Maudie. Wednesday's not Phyll's night to ring. We talk on Fridays. End of the week. Seven o'clock. Regular. That's our time. She and Vic have had their tea by then and we can talk for as long as we like. Or until Vic gets up from the telly and says, 'Are you two still at it? You're a regular pair of gasbags,' good-humoured like.

I don't think he minds. He used to be a bit stand-offish, like he was being careful. I could never work that one out. He's relaxed a bit in the last few years, and since Jack's been gone, Vic's gone out of his way to give me a hand when I've needed it. He's a decent man. I'm glad Phyll ended up with him. He's been a good husband even if he does have some strange ideas.

I look forward to my talks with Phyll. She's always making a joke. She has me in stitches sometimes. I nearly fall off the chair I laugh so much. She's always been like that, the joker of the family. Cheering us up, making us laugh. We used to have some good times around that old kitchen table at Mum's with the whole family there. We'd clear away the dishes at the end of the meal and no one ever wanted to leave. We stayed there talking and telling stories, drinking pot after pot of tea. Even after we were married, we went round there at least once a week. We made our own fun in those days.

It's strange to think that Maudie's on the way out but I suppose at eighty you can't live forever.

PHYLL

What a morning, what with all the rushing and having to sort out Maudie. Then Nell's boat was late and that really set Vic off. It's the parking, you see. You can't stop for more than five minutes in that part of town. Pick up and set down. That's all it is.

Anyway the boat was twenty minutes late so we had to drive around to the Strand and stop there for a bit. Vic's always ready to do a good turn but he does hate being messed about. He gets a bit nervy in traffic. He had to do a U-turn outside the ferry terminus and that sort of thing always sets him off. And then he turns to me and says, 'And for Chrissake, stop that blessed scratching.' Well, what am I supposed to do about it? If I have an itch I have to scratch.

By the time Nell arrived, I'd managed to pretty much jolly him out of it but it took all my effort. And then, wouldn't you believe it, the traffic was banked up going around the hill. He ended up tetchy for the rest of the morning. It's not that he'd snap at anyone, mind – other than me, that is. He just goes very quiet. Nell didn't seem to notice, but with Nell you never can tell whether she just doesn't see things or whether she chooses to overlook them. Nell's always been one for family harmony.

It's like the Casket tickets. 'Keep your money,' I tell her. 'Vic's happy to give a hand. He doesn't want anything for it.' But no, next time she turns up with another one and then Vic gets cross, but with me, not her. 'Tell her to stop buying them,' he says. 'I have,' I say, 'she just ignores me.' She's always been like that. No matter what you say to her, Nell never argues, she just quietly keeps doing things her way.

We took the long way out to the hospital, going round

the hill and down past the old Town Common. I generally like a bit of a drive. It can be really nice on a hot day with the windows down. Mind you, I never was one for staying at home when there was the opportunity to get out and about. I hadn't counted on going past the cemetery, though, and that always makes me feel down. Last time we went there, it was to see to Vic's mother's grave. It was a horrible day, hot and sticky, not a breath of wind, and the two of us digging and weeding and generally tidying up and putting in some plants. I could have done with a quiet sit-down under a tree but we just had to keep going till it was all done. That's Vic's way. 'Get in. Get cracking and the job's over in no time.' And as soon as it is he's off looking for another one. He's never happy sitting still, that man.

There are times when he drives me to distraction but at other times it's like he reads me. The days when I feel like I'm dog-paddling like crazy and my head's just above water and I can't think straight. It's those days he just seems to know I'm struggling and he's there, like a patch of solid earth.

As we drove past the cemetery, Nell said, 'I suppose we should think about the inevitable,' just as I was thinking, Won't be long before we're bringing Maudie back here. Well, it was true. No point beating around the bush. That's why we were all heading to the hospital, to pay our last respects. It's the right thing to do. After all, Maudie's our sister, even if she's past recognising the fact. The problem is, there's no knowing how long she might last. The doctor made that clear over the phone. 'Taken a turn for the worse,' he said. 'She's quite comfortable but I expect the end to come quickly.' I laughed at that. Maudie never lets things end fast.

IRIS

To see us sitting around the bed like this, why, it's just like when we were children, when Maudie had a bit of a chest or another convulsion. It was always one thing or another with Maudie. 'You'll ruin her, Mum,' I used to say. 'She'll grow up fit for nothing.' Mum didn't take any notice. She was always worried about Maudie's health, because of the epilepsy. If she could see her lying here now and see the colour in her cheeks! You'd think she would get up and walk away. For years she's been as fit and healthy as the rest of us. She even managed to hold down a job, which is more than I ever thought Mum would let her do. It's only the stroke that's affected her now. I wouldn't be surprised if she pulled out of it, despite what the doctor says.

Maudie's always been one to get hurt easily. I don't know if it was the convulsions that made her so sensitive but as a child she'd cry easily. One little scratch and she'd be in tears, and she was always banging into things. If there was a door, Maudie would walk into it. She never learnt the knack of walking around or through things. She was a rough little one, despite her ringlets and the sweet expression on her face. When she was older she would get touchy and that sweetness could certainly turn sour. All you had to do was look at her the wrong way and she'd have a fit of pique! I called in to see Mum one day and there was Maudie doing battle with a broom. 'What's up with her?' I asked Mum. 'One of the women at work made a comment and Maudie took it the wrong way,' she said. Maudie had nursed those bruised feelings all the way home and then took her hurt out on every skirting board and stick of furniture that got in the way as she swept the floor.

We used to say the rosary around Maudie's bedside. When Mum didn't want her up in the night chill or walking on the cold floor, we took our books and our needlework and joined her in her bed to keep her company, and every evening we spent the best part of half an hour reciting the rosary. Hail Mary, Holy Mary, Hail Mary, Holy Mary, a decade for this and a decade for that and a decade to keep the family in food and out of strife. Phyll was allowed a cushion to buffer her young knees against the hard wooden boards but Nell and I had to suffer in silence. And Maudie? She got to lie back on soft pillows. I'm sure the prayers didn't earn me any graces, since I was saying them with such mean thoughts and my poor aching knees consumed my mind and my heart. For what it was worth as a consolation, I learnt to be tough and not complain.

It was only us that prayed – us and Mum. Dad never joined in when he was alive on account of his being a member of the Lodge. He used to stand up from the dinner table, sweep the front of his shirt with his napkin, fold it neatly by his plate and wander down to the hammock under the house. There he would light a pipe and swing gently backwards and forwards, listening to the rhythm of our prayers up above. When we had finished and washed our faces and feet, he would come back up the stairs and kiss us each goodnight. I still remember his strong, rough hug and the scent of tobacco lingering about him.

Bedtimes and homecomings were the favourite parts of my day. Each evening, at six o'clock, Nell and I used to run to the end of our street and wait there on the big granite rocks that clustered at the base of the hill. Our part of town was way past the Causeway, out where the town crept along the floodplain, one house, one shed at a time. The main road was no more than a track worn in the dried grass by the drays and buggies as they made their way into and out of town. Graded roads in those parts were still a few years away and every day Dad had a rough bike ride to and from his job running the accounts department at the main Patterson and Parkes warehouse in town. Nell and I would wait for him, looking west from our perch on the rocks, across the plain and over the river to where the sun set. It had a fierce orange glow that ate into your skin right up to the last second before it slipped down behind Mount Stuart.

If he was on time, Dad would appear just as the last light faded. We would throw out our arms to grab him and, with one of us on the seat, the other balanced on the handlebars and both of us clinging to him with great concentration, we'd make our way home together in the shadows.

I missed that when Dad died. Everything changed. We lost our home. We moved to the south side and Nell had to stay at home while Mum went to work. I wanted to start working straight away but Mum insisted I finish my education first so that I could get a job that paid well. I had to be her right hand and share the responsibility of rearing the family. At first Mum took in laundry to support us and she did some housekeeping for an elderly lady nearby, but then she was offered the housekeeper's position at the Criterion Hotel where she'd worked before she was married. She'd always stayed friendly with Mrs Chambers, the publican's wife, and sometimes when we were in town she would take us to have fresh lemon squash in the ladies' lounge. Housekeepers generally worked long hours but Mrs Chambers agreed that Mum could take some of the sewing home where Nell and I could give a hand.

Mum seemed to need more than a few prayers to help persuade her she could keep the family going and that's where our knees went to work. The prayers must have paid off in the end because Nell and I got good jobs and made good wages that went towards helping Mum with the household expenses. I don't know whether things would have been much different had Dad been alive. Easier maybe, but not much different. Look at Evie Crow's family. She had a dad but he was mostly out of work. We were only a family of women but we did all right. It taught us to bear up and be strong. There's no point expecting others to feel pity for you. Pity doesn't put food on the table every night, or pay the electric light, or keep a roof over your head. You have to take charge and do the right thing, even if it's inconvenient. You have to be careful, to make the best of your situation and not leave yourself open to criticism. We've been lucky. Our lives have turned out all right in the end. Even Phyll's. She met young Vic and he's been a good support all right. He was always polite although he's never been especially warm toward me. He softened up a bit after Bill died but he was just being kind, I suppose, on account of my being a widow.

KATE

From as early as I can remember, I've been fascinated by conversations. Whenever my mother stopped to share the local news and gossip, outside the school gate, down at the shops, or in front of the church after Mass on Sunday mornings, I would dip in and out of the adults' conversations. Suddenly I would realise that the chat was all about something new, and time and again I would ask Mum why this was so. 'The conversation's changed,' she would reply.

'How did that happen?'

'I don't know. Someone just started telling a new story.'

'How did they know you'd all finished with the old one?'

'Katey, where on earth do you find these questions?'

Her attempts to dismiss the subject were as futile as her attempts to explain it, and for quite some time I would sit on the edge of my mother's conversations, concentrating hard, trying to be there right at the moment when it changed.

One day, around the time my cousin Gayle had her third son, I was listening in as Mum, Nana and Maudie were sitting at Nana's kitchen table discussing the baptism. All the family were going to Auntie Iris's for morning tea instead of coming back to Nana's after church, as we usually did on Sunday morning.

'Are Phyll and Vic coming?' asked Maudie.

'I didn't ask,' said Mum.

'They never go to Iris's place and no one else ever goes to theirs.'

Mum cut her short. 'It's their business, Maudie.'

Maudie wouldn't let up. 'They should sort this out. It's gone on too long.'

Nana looked at my comic book lying open and unread on the table in front of me as I listened intently to the three women. She lifted the lid on the aluminium teapot and pushed the pot towards Maudie.

Maudie's exasperation flew across the table in an explosion of breath. She flung her chin forward into the cup of her palm and fixed her gaze on Nana. Then she threw her shoulders back, slammed her palms onto the tabletop and stood, scraping the chair legs loudly over the floorboards. The chair struck the kitchen dresser with a crash, rattling the plates and rocking the cups on their hooks. Mum grabbed a corner of the dresser to steady it but Maudie seemed oblivious to the near calamity. Her voice shook as she declared, 'I am *not* making any more tea,' and she stormed out of the room.

Later, during the course of one of the lengthy afternoon conversations that Mum and I used to have about nothing in particular, Mum let slip that there was a time when Auntie Iris and Auntie Phyll didn't talk. It was nothing serious, she said, just a misunderstanding that got out of hand. Poor Nana, she said. Poor Nana got blamed for it.

I couldn't imagine anyone blaming Nana for anything. It wasn't that she did anything in particular to make you like her. She just seemed to watch and to know and to understand. If Nana said you should do something, you did it, not because you were forced to but because you believed she would always give the right advice. I certainly couldn't believe that Nana's own daughters would chastise her.

Eventually Mum let on that Auntie Iris and Auntie Phyll had gone away on holiday together, to a farm near Tully. It was a surprise to me since I had hardly ever seen the two of them in one room at the same time. The only time I remember them being together was at Nana's funeral. After the burial we all went back to Nana's house, where everyone discussed whether Maudie should stay on living there – everyone, that is, except Maudie, who was busy going backwards and forwards to the kitchen making tea. Auntie Phyll got really upset and started to sob. Mum rubbed one finger briskly against the opposite hand. Without a word, Auntie Iris stood up and walked outside.

NELL

I was waiting for the others in Maudie's hospital room when it happened.

The nice nurse helps me outside, the young one. Her name is May. I wondered where she was from, then one day I heard her talking about the Philippines. She helps me out to the verandah and fetches me a glass of water, so I can take the aspirin. 'I sometimes take a turn and my doctor says this will help to ward it off,' I say, as if I need to explain myself. 'Don't make a fuss. I don't want to worry the others.' She takes my hand as if to soothe me and I look away. Kate holds my hand like this. Generally, people are kind to me but as for holding hands and touching, well, that's something you do with your own people. I suppose it reminds me how much I would like to have Kate here. You do, you know. You start to feel a bit like . . . Oh, I don't know. I just don't have the same sort of energy for going out. I'm too old to drag myself all around town. I'd like to have my daughter to rely on the way Iris has her Gayle. I get lonely and tired. When you live by yourself, you have to go out for company. You have to make the effort. I've got to the stage where I just want to be in my own home with my own flesh and blood doing for me and not be forced to rely on strangers.

May. That's what she said her name was. She lets go of my hand and leans back against the verandah railing. 'You remind me of my grandmother.' Well, I never! I laugh at that one. 'No,' she says, 'My grandmother has a big family but none of her daughters live near her. It's very sad.' Sad! That's the word for it all right. But there's no point brooding on it. You have to get on with life. Whether you're happy or sad, the kitchen floor will still need sweeping. That's what Mum used to say.

I sometimes wonder which of us will be the last to go. We always expected Maudie to be the first. Phyll is the youngest but that's no guarantee she'll outlast Iris. I can't imagine life without Iris. It was just the two of us, in the beginning. We grew up together. We did things at the same time and in much the same way. Phyll was a lot younger. She always went off and did things her own way. As for Maudie, she didn't do much of anything at all, especially without Mum's say so. Iris and I were older and we were reliable so I suppose Mum trusted us with jobs. She had to. After Dad died there wasn't much option. She needed all the help she could get.

'Is your husband here?' May asked. Her eyes were so full of concern I would have laughed again if it hadn't been for the fact that she reminded me about Jack. I lost him six years ago now. It felt like we'd hardly started our retirement and he was gone. You work hard, raise a family, and when you finally get to enjoy the fruits of your labour it's all over. Iris was a big support when he died. She had lost Bill the year before so it was all very fresh for her. After the funeral, after Kate and the boys had left and before the flowers had started to wilt, she came over to the Island. Every fortnight for a couple of months she'd bunk down for a few days in Jack's old bed in the back room. It was where he used to have his afternoon sleep, out there in the three-quarter bed. We brought it over with some other pieces of his mother's furniture after she died.

Having Iris move about the house helped to fill that big empty space. It gave me something to look forward to, knowing she'd be coming over, and when she was there her snores filtered through those still moments at daybreak when I'd wake and realise how empty the bed was without Jack's big bones to fill it.

We were only a few months short of our golden wedding anniversary when he passed away. All the children had made plans to come home, except Kate. She hated to commit to any of these things but she'd always turn up at the last minute, walking through the back door, a big grin on her face, saying, 'Bet you didn't think you'd see me here.' Kate's my youngest. I suppose I was too soft on her in the beginning but she was a late baby and she used to be so easy to handle when she was little. That all changed later. As she got older she could be difficult at times.

We spent weeks planning the party. Jack did most of the work, getting the garden up to scratch, ordering the food and drink, and even writing the invitations while I was out at my bridge afternoons. He was real keen on having a marquee and celebrating with the crowd that we mixed with in the old days on the south side.

That was a grand old group. We had maybe twenty or thirty regulars. We met at the church social club, played tennis, went to dances and parties together and saw each other at Mass on Sundays. We did everything in big groups then. There was none of this dating rubbish. We got to know each other properly before we announced our intentions. Jack courted me for three years before he proposed. Our friends all got married around the same time. We went to each other's weddings and pooled our cash to buy each couple a decent present for setting up a home. Once the babies started to come along we drifted apart, but that was to be expected with people moving out to new parishes and money going into buying the family home and raising the children.

The year I turned sixty-four and Jack was sixty-five, the funerals began. One morning he looked up from his breakfast and said, 'Alec O'Rourke's gone. His funeral notice is in the paper.' Well, Alec and Jack went way back, to the yacht squadron in the thirties when they sailed the 18-footers out of Ross Creek on Sunday afternoons. That started it. From then on it seemed like we had a funeral every second week, this one's husband and that one's wife. Jack said it was like reliving the war, never knowing who was going to fall off the perch next. We ran into people we hadn't seen for years but we were such a sad bunch. You could hardly raise a smile out of any of us. That's how the anniversary parties began. It was an excuse to cheer us all up, make us feel like there was something to look forward to amongst all this remembering. Except we didn't make our golden. I had to organise Jack's funeral instead.

May touches my shoulder. 'How are you feeling now?' Her dark hair gleams against the crisp whiteness of her nurse's cap.

'I'm fine,' I say, a bit too quickly. To tell the truth she startled me. When I get to thinking about Jack, everything else just seems to slip away.

IRIS

I don't know why Bill was the way he was. He couldn't stick at anything for very long, always changing jobs. He took care of the family. He was never out of work. As soon as he walked out of one position, another opened up for him. The pay was always adequate. It's just that he was never satisfied. In fact, he was downright dissatisfied. He was a moody man all right, never happy with anything. He could work hard but he was impatient and the rewards never came fast enough for him, so he'd pack up and move on, but never without having an argument first. It was like he always had to burn his bridges. He couldn't bring himself to do it quietly. He had to leave under a cloud, blaming somebody else for why it didn't work out.

The bad moods always came home to me. He wasn't easy to live with, that's for sure, but you marry somebody and that's the way it is. Good or bad, you have to put up with it. There was no point complaining or talking to him about it. Luckily, I was made of stern stuff. I could bear the brunt of it without arguing back. He had a fierce temper if you stoked it. I wasn't ready to put the children and myself in the line of fire. Better to keep things sweet and wait for him to come round. Once he got over a mood he'd be a decent man until the next one. He never touched the children. Never laid a hand on them. Sometimes I feared he might get rough with me but no, his tongue was his weapon, and a cruel one it was at that. He could cut you into pieces with one look and a sharp word.

It wasn't so bad at the beginning. I suppose I just happened to meet him in happy circumstances. I was doing the accounts at Carroll's, the department store, and Bill was delivering for one of the wholesalers. He had just started the job so he was in good spirits, but when I look back on it the moods were always there. We didn't spend enough time alone in each other's company for it to really become noticeable, and I suppose when you start out fresh, with high hopes, you overlook these things. It only got bad once the pattern was set, when he realised he wasn't going anywhere and wasn't likely to either. That's when things got nasty. Bill had big plans, big dreams, but they came to nothing. He couldn't bring himself to stick with something for long enough to see it all come together.

What made it worse was seeing Jack do so well. Bill and Jack started out together and then Bill got Jack the position at Cummins and Campbell. It wasn't Jack's fault that Bill left, but leave he did and next thing, Jack's got the junior salesman's position. Before long he's the town traveller and doing very nicely on commission. Oh, for sure, there were times when things were tight for Nell and him, especially after they bought that place at the Island. Mum let on to me once about Nell having to pinch pennies to make ends meet and I certainly did my share of handing things on for the children. Well, we're family, Nell and I, and between us there's never been any jealousy. It only came about with Jack doing so well and Bill feeling he was missing out. I can't say there weren't times when I felt envious, especially after things got easier for them, but Jack worked hard. He grabbed opportunities that came his way and made the most of them. It's a pity he wasn't around for very long after he retired to enjoy it all. Mind you, he left Nell very comfortable and that's what counts.

Nell and I are close again now that we're both widows. Our lives followed pretty much the same paths. There's only fourteen months between us so it's natural we grew up close. For years Mum had a studio photo of the two of us on the table in her sitting room, taken before the others came along. We must have been six and seven years old at most, standing straight, holding hands. I had a slight advantage in height and Nell's dark hair and eyes stood out next to my lighter hazelnut looks. Our hair was a mass of loosely coiled ringlets. It makes me laugh to remember Mum setting it every night, winding it up in strips of old sheeting and releasing it into shining coils in the morning. Our dresses were starched white cotton with rows and rows of pin tucking and ruching that she sewed by hand in perfect lines of evenly spaced stitches. It's a wonder she didn't go blind doing such fine needlework with only a kerosene lamp to see by.

Nell comes over every second Thursday. She catches the ferry and then comes all the way out here by bus. It's a pleasure to see her. Sometimes she brings pikelets for afternoon tea and sometimes we just sit and talk. We used to stroll over to the nursing ward to spend an hour or so with Maudie, even though she was losing her memory. Most days she didn't even recognise us. This stroke is a blessing really, if she goes quickly.

PHYLL

The year Vic and I moved to Tully it was 1948, and Tully was the wettest place in Australia.

Vic thought I didn't want to leave Mum while I was expecting. He thought a woman would need her mother at a time like that. I couldn't tell him I had been through it all before. That was too shameful to admit and, anyway, Mum said I should put it all behind me. Things had turned out for the best, she said, and when I met Vic after the war I believed she was right. There was no point burdening him with things that were over and done with.

For the first two months in Tully it rained every day, sheets of rain. Heavy, drenching rain you couldn't walk through. It fell at all times of the day. You could never predict it. I would go out in bright sunshine to walk a half a mile to the corner store and before I was halfway there the skies would open and down it would come. Give it ten or fifteen minutes and the clouds would clear and out would come the sun again, bright and strong and turning the place into a steam bath. I was wet for the whole two years we lived up there. Nothing ever dried. Our wedding photos stuck to each other and mould grew in dark corners without invitation.

Vic was a traveller with Burns Philp. He worked out of the Tully office, visiting all the stores in the area, taking their orders and sending them off to the main office in Townsville. If there were any problems with the orders when they arrived, Vic was the man who had to sort it all out. The job suited him, always rushing about doing this thing or that for people; he liked being busy and being necessary. In Tully he got to run his own show. It was a good opportunity – I couldn't ask him to turn it down, and how would I have explained it?

You couldn't really call Tully a town. It was more like a cluster of houses around the mill and a main street of shops that ran crookedly into the side of the range. We rented a house on the rise at the foot of the mountain, a short distance from the main street. The house was an ordinary Queenslander – two main rooms, an open verandah that ran around three sides and an enclosed back verandah where we could eat next to the kitchen, and there was a lean-to bathroom. The back of the house sat in the slope of the mountain, and a set of steps, hacked into the solid red clay, led up to the outside toilet which you could only just see from the main house. The rainforest shaded the house and kept the inside cool and moist, even when the clouds cleared enough to let the tropical sun shine through.

The mill was the heart and soul of Tully. During the cane-cutting season you had the noise of the crushers day and night, except when it was broken by the whistle that marked the end of one shift and the beginning of the next. When we arrived in town, I was four months gone with our first son and I spent a lot of time sitting in the cane chair on the front verandah, sewing and mending, but mostly just sitting. I could see down across the gully to the mill gates where, day and night for weeks on end, the cane trains steamed in with a full load and out again with empty bins. At the end of their shifts, even if it was eleven o'clock in the morning, the men streamed out of the gates and across the road to the front bar of the Great Northern. There was always a huge racket coming from that place during trading hours and you could tell when closing time came because the noise of drunken scuffles on the street would carry across the gully and in through the open windows of the house.

At night I sat out there on the verandah listening to the regular chunk and grind of the crushers and the belligerent voices, and the low rumble from less argumentative comrades wandering off into the night. I sat there and thought of my baby until the persistent whine of mosquitoes drove me back to the protection of the net and the clammy air inside.

Although our place was close to the top end of the main street, there was only one other house nearby. A Maltese family lived there. Vic struck up a friendship with the father, a young man called Joe who worked at the mill. Vic was good at making friends. He was curious about people and he never hesitated to approach them. He found out very quickly that Joe's dream was to have a cane farm that he could pass on to his sons.

I used to see Maria, Joe's wife, coming and going

during the day as she took the children to and from school, and in the middle of the day she carried Joe's meal down to him at the mill. Maria's mother was always at home, washing or cooking or tending to the vegetables she planted, laying them out in neat rectangular gardens in the front of the house. Mrs Calleja had travelled with the family from Malta and sometimes, like when Joe wandered in late from the pub, I would hear her talking to him loudly in Maltese and I wondered who made the rules in the household.

If anyone had asked, I couldn't have explained why I started walking. It was idleness and restlessness at the same time. I know that's a contradiction but it's how I felt. I had no energy to start things and less desire to finish them but I hated to sit around the house. I felt shut in and the moisture-laden air sat heavy on me. I needed to feel myself moving and have air flowing into my lungs. That's when I started walking.

I left the house with nothing, not even an umbrella. The doors were open and the dinner slowly stewing on the stove. I left by the back stairs and pushed my way out through the overgrown yard to the dirt track that led to the top of the main street. By the time I reached it, a soft mist of rain was already settling over the town. I remember that I crossed quickly and went into the bush on the other side. I had no plan, no place to end up. I just needed to move.

I didn't intend to visit the church. I came into the clearing from the back and I was already halfway round the side of the building before I recognised the place. It was made of timber and its short wooden stumps were capped with iron to keep the white ants out, which gave it the amusing appearance of an elegant lady with her nose in the air, lifting her skirts and picking her way on tiptoe across a patch of mud. The church sat in a clearing that had been roughly hacked from the rainforest and already the bracken was edging back to reclaim its territory. A Moreton Bay fig had been planted to one side of the ground, so long ago that its branches made a canopy that covered most of the space. Even it could not hold back the rain that was now falling steadily. I circled the church hoping to find an overhanging piece of roof to shelter me. That's when I saw the cemetery.

I had seen it before, on Sunday mornings when Vic and I came to Mass, but with him there and the rest of the congregation casting an eye over the newcomers, I couldn't walk over and search in amongst the graves even if I'd wanted to. The aerial roots that anchored the tree had grown down amongst the headstones so that the older ones were bound in strange tangles. I can't explain why I had this sudden urge to find the place because, up until then, I'd pushed anything to do with it right to the back of my mind. The grave was over to one side of the consecrated ground, next to a newly built fence. It was tiny and unmarked and I only found it because of the way the earth was built up in a rectangular mound, edged with stones, just as Uncle Denny said he had done.

I stayed there for an age, my knees cushioned in the soft wet soil. I didn't cry. It was cool in the shade of the fig tree and, when the drizzle stopped, a breeze swept through the clearing and raised the hairs on my arms. Then the mill siren sounded and I turned down the road leading up from the town and walked home.

I must have walked miles over the next few months. Even as I grew bigger and my movements became restricted, I still walked each day, and each walk seemed to lead to the churchyard. There was a rock that was about the right size for me to rest on, neither sitting nor standing but able to take the weight off my feet. I could stay there for an hour or more, never seeing anyone, just staring at the cemetery where my baby lay. The air seemed to flow more freely than at the house. It was fresher and I could breathe more easily.

One afternoon I came back later than usual. I must have missed the siren, and as I approached the house, Mrs Calleja was standing at the front verandah with her daughter. Words that I couldn't understand spilled from her lips and she spoke so quickly I couldn't tell whether she was speaking Maltese or broken English. Maria interrupted her.

'My mother worried you had accident.'

'No. I'm all right.' I didn't think anyone had noticed my comings and goings.

Mrs Calleja put one hand to her stomach and spoke again. Maria turned to me. 'She says your baby comes soon. When you need us, we will help.'

Peter was born very quickly in the bedroom that opened onto the wide verandah of the house. I was out of bed the day after the birth but I had no energy to care for him. More than that, I had no will. I didn't want to touch him, I didn't want to hold him. I could hardly bear to nurse him. It was a great relief when the doctor ordered me to express milk and feed him from a bottle. I did everything I had to, but there was no feeling for him. For months the underneath of the house was like a forest with lines strung with wet nappies. Some days I tried ironing them to dry the dampness out of them. It didn't help. It wasn't just the rain; the moisture was in the air, it was in everything. It was an effort to move, let alone look after this baby – bathe him, change him, rock him. Even to touch him was an effort. I struggled from one task to another and, in between, I paced the floor, backwards and forwards, across the front verandah.

One day I just walked out. By the time I got back, it was late afternoon and shadows were falling across the road. Mrs Calleja was making her way through the long grass to her house. Vic stood on the verandah, his hand on the side of Peter's crib. He watched me come up the stairs.

I was in a dark place. I couldn't look at my son. I tried to hold him, but I shook all over.

Vic showed his true colours then. Mrs Calleja took Vic aside and talked with him. I don't know exactly what she said but it was after that he stepped in and took over. The groceries came through the company. Orders for meat and fresh food went in every week and were delivered to the house. Vic paid Mrs Calleja to housekeep. In the afternoons she sat with Peter while I walked for miles along the old cedar-getters' tracks through the rainforest, and on the worst days Vic sent word to the office to say he wouldn't be in and he stayed at home to take care of Peter.

When I saw the pleasure Vic took in his son, I didn't know what to feel. There was relief that my baby was loved and cared for, but there was anger and sadness and this awful despair. The inside of my head would go numb. I was frightened then, frightened of being left alone with my son, frightened of what I might do without realising it.

KATE

There's no reason not to go. I can get time off work.

I think Dan's okay about me being away. He hasn't asked me not to go. I'm glad to be going to the Island. I need time to rest, time to think and the chance to be myself again. Yet I hesitate before picking up the phone to make the call. The summer sunshine floods into the room and reflects in the pale gold of the apple cider in my glass.

There's a mist of condensation around the outside and the ice cubes are melting fast.

We chose this apartment because it has uninterrupted views of the sun as it sets over the western suburbs. We can see across the top end of the city and the light industrial buildings of the inner west and all the way up to where the plains flatten out on either side of the river. In the distance are the mountains. It's not the million-dollar harbour view that people associate with Sydney but it suits me fine, and on certain days during the year the sun glows burnt orange just before it slips down behind the Great Divide. Dan says it's the pollution but we still love to sit and look at it.

I like to study the sun as it sets and ponder the way we say it is setting when it is really the earth that is rising. When I tell that to Dan, he laughs at me.

'Why on earth do you bother?'

'It's true.' I leap from the sofa. 'It completely changes the way you look at things.'

Dan pulls me back. 'All right. All right. Don't be so defensive.'

'I have to be with you around, you big bully.' I push him over and straddle him, pinning him to the sofa.

'You can bully me instead.' He gives a wicked laugh.

'It's not the right time. You have to save yourself for a couple more days.'

'No way, honey. Today we're on holidays from that.' He rolls gently onto his side, toppling me into the space next to him. His body pushes me up against the sofa cushions as he stokes my leg. 'This one's just for you and me.'

Afterwards Dan lies sprawled across me, warm and smelling of sex. I push my face into his and breathe in his scent. He stirs for a moment and loosens the hand that still cups my breast. My arm drifts down his back, stroking the muscles that have gone soft in sleep, and I dream of lying here forever. I think of the program. Am I ready to have a baby? I know I want it but could I really be a good mother?

It seems that in the space of a single, simple moment the sun has gone and the city darkness is penetrated by thousands of little lights. I feel crushed and I push gently at Dan to roll his sleeping body away from me without waking him. But it's not him that's weighing me down. The space inside the apartment is pressing in on me and my lungs can't expand to take breath. I leave the room in darkness and make my way down the hall to the bathroom. My eyes are accustomed to the lack of light and I have no trouble finding my way. In the darkness I can manage.

It will be good to get away. Get some space. Sort out the little voices that creep in at the sides of my head. I want things to be right. I want to be sure.

I take the phone into the bedroom to make the call.

'I was just thinking of you.' Her voice on the end of the line is reassuring. 'I'm here by myself, doing the vegetables for dinner. Vic went to collect Phyll from the hospital.' She gives me an activity-by-activity report of their day. Mum did the morning visit, Phyll did the afternoon and Gayle will go up this evening. Iris doesn't go every day on account of not being so good on her legs and finding it hard to move about.

'I'm flying up on Monday.'

'That's good news, Kate. I'm pleased.'

I'll catch a cab from the airport, I tell her, knowing Vic will come to pick me up but wanting to leave it open so he doesn't feel it's expected. We organise the trip and she says, 'I'll let you go then. I can't monopolise your time.' I tell her, 'It's all right. Dan's asleep. What are you doing about your bridge club?' I ask her questions with answers that don't really matter, just to keep her talking, to fill the distance between us. The ordinariness of it all helps to calm the spinning in my head and I settle into a slump on the bed.

'There's one thing I should tell you.'

My back snaps straight. She's done it again. In the middle of a simple conversation, she throws in a few words that leave me hanging. I don't need the suspense but I hold my breath to make her fill the space.

'It's Gayle,' she says. 'She's left her husband.'

Gayle, my mid-fifties, respectable cousin who has always fulfilled the family's expectations!

'I won't say any more. I just wanted you to know before you got here.'

When the call is over, I sit back in the dark and watch the lights. It takes a long time for the apartment walls to move back into place and for my breathing to be steady again.

Gayle was a young mother with two lively sons when she and Auntie Iris came to visit us on the Island. Auntie Iris and Mum babysat, leaving Gayle free to explore the Island, and she would take me on her expeditions. I suppose I must have been company, though we hardly spoke. On the first afternoon, we wandered down through the gully at the end of our street where the river snakes a thin line through the guinea grass. We were only a few steps from home but, in my mind, we were on a great trek that would take us over the southern point and down to the boulder-strewn cove we called Rocky Bay. I loved to make this trek but I rarely had the chance to do it once my brothers left home. It was on this walk that I began my fantasy about Gayle being my mother. She was so pretty, with her short bobbed hair and matador pants, just like the mothers on TV. My own mother was old, older than all the other mothers I knew.

Gayle was quiet and thoughtful as we walked. The trail we followed was a thin line worn by the feet of day-trekkers but I preferred to imagine that we were the first. We were hunters in search of prey. We were shipwrecked sailors in search of a place to make our camp. We were a beautiful young mother and her daughter, in search of our husband and father who had gone missing on an overland exploration. To me, Gayle's husband was just a shadowy figure in her background, so I was free to paint my own picture of my perfect dad.

The walk up was hot. Moving fast in the still of mid-afternoon when the day was at its hottest brought a coating of sweat to my skin. The moisture gathered in the crease of my elbows and it started to itch, but I knew that later Mum would rub sweet-smelling calamine lotion onto my irritated skin to ease the inflammation. On the lower slope our footsteps raised a fine black dust which stuck to the dampness around my feet. Further up, as the climb grew steeper, the track became firmer until it was like climbing a staircase of rocks. As we clambered like goats around giant granite boulders, my chest burned with the effort of keeping the pace.

All of a sudden the trees thinned and the wind struck us. It came straight off the sea and, after the stillness and heat, it felt like ice against my burning skin. I ran ahead to reach the open sunlight and warmth. The wind grabbed and tore at my straw hat so fiercely it was only saved by the piece of thin elastic that now threatened to choke me. The long grasses covering the headland were laid flat by the constant force. We stood for a few moments looking out to sea and letting the warmth of the sun on one side counter the chill of the wind on the other. The sea was the rich colour that I have since learnt to associate with this place, set at that point where blue becomes green and right before your eyes slips back into blue. The day that had seemed so still was now whipped to a frenzy, with white caps scattered across the tops of the waves. I was surprised to see the water so disturbed.

The giant waves, thundering in from the open sea, break on the main beds of the Great Barrier Reef that lie further to the east. Here on the Island, where we sit close to the coast surrounded by small reefs, the sea is more usually calm. From our jetty, there are only five miles across the channel to the harbour opening, and I have experienced night crossings of the channel on an ancient wooden ferry that have taught me the force of the currents that swell and flow around us.

Looking south-west across the channel I could see the mainland at Cape Bowling Green. It was a thin outline of coast, flat for a distance then rising steeply to the mountains of the Great Divide. Further around, the sea met the sky in a bright haze and I wondered why it wasn't possible to see more. Gayle was silent. She stood nearby, just staring outward. Then she turned towards the track that led down into Rocky Bay and, without speaking, I followed.

With a few steps, we were out of the wind and into the humidity again. There was no bush on this side but the arm of the headland protected us. The slope here was so steep and gravelly, it was hard to keep from slipping and sliding on your bottom nearly all the way to the beach. The excitement of the drop thrilled me and, with the natural agility of a child, I leapt from outcrop to outcrop, using the momentum to propel me towards the nearest platform and bouncing off it to the next. In a few moments I was standing triumphantly in the sand. Gayle slipped and let out a shriek, grabbing for a handhold. She eyed the distance between us and groaned.

'How do we get back up?'

'There's a track on the other side. It goes up to the road.'

She studied the small ridge that ran through the middle of the bay and separated it into canyons. From where we were on the headland side it hid the second track.

'You'd better be right, kiddo.'

She picked her way gingerly from rock to grass tuft, anchoring herself at intervals on her bottom to keep her balance until she finally reached the beach. She sank onto the finely ground sand and let out a long breath. 'Do you do that often?'

'Not since Gerry went away. Mum doesn't like the track.'

'I'm not surprised. I can't see my mum getting down there in one piece.' She scooped up a handful of sand and let it run out. I wanted us to jump up and explore the beach together. I wanted us to swim in the breakers that Mum had ruled out of bounds in case of sharks. I wanted us to search for sand dollars along the shoreline, where the water played a game of advancing and retreating and advancing further up the beach in ever increasing arcs of wetness.

Gayle just sat there studying the pattern the sand made as it fell through her fingers.

I spoke, as much to reclaim her attention as to elicit information. 'Mum says you're good at drawing.'

'I did graphic art at school.'

'Do you still do it?'

She wiped her palm across the sand, smoothing out the surface, and with one finger she drew an outline. 'There's not much time with the boys.'

'Do you need a lot of time to do art?' It didn't seem to me that drawing something should take much time out of a day.

Some of the composure seemed to fall away from Gayle's face, leaving her cloaked in a sadness I could not decipher. She just sat there, watching the waves wash in and out. Then, as if she were suddenly aware that her mood was settling on me, she pressed the soles of her feet into the sand and pushed herself upright. 'Come on,' she said, 'if we find nice shells we can take them home for drawing.'

GAYLE

I never would have picked Katey to be the rebellious one, certainly not when she was young and always hanging about the house with Auntie Nell. She was not at all like those boisterous big brothers of hers. Auntie Nell didn't encourage her going off with other children. 'You can't be too careful,' she used to say over and over again. 'It's all right with boys, but with girls you can't be too careful.'

I can't say that I agreed with her but since I didn't have a daughter of my own, there was no point in arguing, and, really, it was not my place to interfere.

We didn't spend a lot of time together, despite being family. When my brothers and I were young, we lived in a house with a huge backyard full of mango trees and, once, Auntie Nell brought Gerry and Graham over to play. The two of them immediately scampered up the trees with my brothers to fight some imaginary battle and reappeared with Graham sporting a broken arm. Whenever Mum mentioned Auntie Nell, she always added, 'I don't know how she manages with those boys. They're a handful.' Kate was the surprise addition, born when Auntie Nell was in her forties. She was only five years older than my own children.

One year Mum and I took the boys on holiday to the Island. Auntie Nell and Uncle Jack's place was a holiday hut set on the flat of the bay amongst a thin forest of gums. A straggly track led up from the beach and from the top step all you could see through the bush were glints of sunlight on the iron roofs of neighbouring huts. A resident kookaburra came each day in search of scraps of meat and at dusk the trees went crazy with the squawking and chatter of birds nesting for the night. It was very different from my high-blocked timber house on a suburban street in an estate of similar houses, separated from each other only by low hedges of red and white bottlebrush trees. Occasionally a flock of galahs descended to pick the grass seeds but mostly the new homeowners kept their grass cut low and the bushes so neatly trimmed that native wildfowl were not encouraged to visit.

Katey was a shy little girl with short dark hair that was cut so the curls fell around her ears. Her eyes looked out at you with the same earnest gaze I had noticed in photos of Auntie Nell and Mum as young girls. At first she held back behind her mother, but from the moment they met us at the jetty, you could see her curiosity in the way she watched and listened to everything we did.

Even though Auntie Nell and Uncle Jack had had the hut on the Island for many years, our family had not visited before. Dad had fixed ideas about some things and taking advantage of family was something he objected to strongly. He didn't like Mum imposing on relatives and his interpretation of imposing included asking to rent the hut for school holidays. He knew that it would be offered for free and Dad hated accepting favours from Uncle Jack.

I loved the place from the moment we set foot on the jetty. It felt like we were in the bush and immediately I wanted to find the drawing things I had left unused for so long.

The hut was comfortable for a bush holiday and built compactly so it could be locked up quickly at the end of a weekend. There was a dormitory in the enclosed front verandah with six beds lined up alongside each other, each with one end to the wall. The roof was unlined so that when you lay there you looked straight at the underneath of the corrugated iron. During the day you could hear the slow creaking from the sheets of iron as they expanded in the heat. The inside of the hut was dim and cool since there were no windows and the ventilation came from shutters that were propped open with a piece of timber. The middle of the building had a small sitting room and, through a curtained doorway, a small changing room that was the only private place in the house. There was no electricity on the Island so the house was lit with kerosene lamps hung from two-inch nails hammered at an angle into the walls. Running the width of the building at the back was a dining room where a huge table took up most of the space, along with benches that could accommodate at least twelve people. A couple of cement steps led down to a lean-to kitchen where the old wood stove used to be. Our only water supply was from rainwater tanks, so we bathed the boys in a tin tub set up in the kitchen, and one corner of the room was partitioned off for the bush shower that we rigged up once a week for ourselves. The rest of the time we stayed clean with an evening wash and a couple of buckets of water thrown over us to rinse off the salt from our daily swim.

We went to the beach in the mornings before the sun got too hot, and even though there were other children there Katey didn't play with them. She stayed close to us and was great at amusing the boys. Chris was three and Brent had just started crawling. Together, they were a handful. I suppose I was impractical but I hadn't expected marriage and children to take over my life as they did. Noel and I didn't plan. We got married. We bought a house. We had children. We raised them. Everyone did the same. If I had considered how all-consuming it would be, I probably would never have done it, especially not with Noel. Mum and I didn't speak about these things but, without being asked, she often took the boys off my hands, and at the Island Katey surprised me with the way she threw herself, heart and soul, into building sandcastles with them and keeping them occupied.

After the beach we would wander slowly back along the esplanade to the general store where we bought ice-cream from a storekeeper who greeted us each day like we were his favourite customers. We sat at the picnic trestles along the beachfront to eat the cones before they melted, but even with four of us fussing over them, the boys always ended up in a sticky mess.

When lunch was out of the way, Auntie Nell always sat at the dining-room table, adding some fine detail to yet another pretty frock for Katey who sat nearby piecing together the left-over scraps of material into clothes for her dolls. Every so often, her mother called her over to check her sewing and help her out with the difficult bits, and Katey leant against her as she followed her experienced fingers twisting and shaping the fabric to achieve the right effect.

Katey's birthday was at the end of our first week on the Island and Mum gave her a pair of yellow cotton shorts with a matching gingham top. She tried them on immediately and came out of the changing room with her cheeks flushed pink and looking plainer and firmer than the young girl who had been wearing the pretty sunsuits that Auntie Nell chose for her. She wanted to wear her new outfit every day and Auntie Nell had to wash it out overnight.

With Mum and Auntie Nell keeping a close watch on the boys, I was finally able to have some time to myself. All my interests, my sketching and painting, had gone by the wayside when I got married and I was happy to have time to do nothing. I took to walking, following unmarked tracks in the bush, with no idea of where they might take me. It was good to have Katey with me since she knew where most of the tracks led. She was a perfect companion, quiet and unobtrusive, leaving me to the thoughts that drifted in and out of my mind.

KATE

Every morning during their visit, we went swimming in the public enclosure. The swimming spot was at the end of the beach where the huge granite boulders tumbled into the sea. The waves crashed against them and every so often, when a ferry circled the reef on its approach to the jetty, its wash would surge against the rocks and suck the beach back and then surge forward again. Lifesavers had enclosed the section with long pieces of railway line, upended and sunk into the sand, making a kind of sharkproof fence through which the sea could flow freely. As the sun rose higher, the boulders threw broad shadows onto the sand, giving plenty of spots to escape from the burning heat. With the noise of it all, it was possible to cocoon yourself completely in that corner as hours just drifted by.

By mid-morning the serious suntanners arrived and we packed up our things to head home. Mum and Auntie Iris dried the boys while Gayle and I went to change. Two changing sheds were built up against the boulders, about ten feet apart. On busy days mumbled conversations and swelling laughter spilled out of the old wooden constructions. Both sheds had wide gaps between the floorboards so the sand and water could spill through, and the local children would scour the sand under the sheds for coins that had fallen from the pockets of careless changers. My brothers skited that they had regularly supplemented their pocket money with their lucrative pickings.

The ladies' shed was windowless. Inside was one open space, lit dimly as the sunlight struggled to penetrate the space between the walls and the ceiling. Rough wooden benches ran along the walls and another split the open space down the centre. Some enterprising soul had hammered two-inch nails into the walls at odd intervals so you could hang up your clothes. The sense of this didn't dawn on me until the day my underpants fell through the gap in the floor and I had to crawl through the pee-drenched sand underneath the building to retrieve them.

One morning Gayle walked into the shed and hung her robe on a nail. She took her towel and held it discreetly against her body with one hand, using the other to peel off her wet togs. As she stepped out of them, her foot caught in the strap and she stumbled against the bench, dropping the towel. Her breasts bounced softly as she landed. She was small-boned and rounded without being muscular and her breasts sat against her body like two soft fruit gently slung in sacs. They were real breasts, soft and pliable, with full nipples. I had seen big, well-corseted bosoms and high-pointed bodices on fashionably dressed young women but never before a whole breast. Mum had a discreet, flat chest. So did Auntie Iris. I had studied the two pink spots on my chest, not holding out much hope for them to develop into anything of significance. Now before me was a vision of what I could become.

Gayle leant down to retrieve the towel, quickly pulling it up to cover herself. She ran an eye over my wet costume as she pulled her beach robe around her. 'You should dry yourself off. It gets chilly when you're out of the sun.' She rubbed one foot against the other in an attempt to dislodge the crusty ridge of sand from around their edges.

'Here,' she said, grabbing her towel, rolling it a few times and tying the corners into a knot. Then she twisted me around and held my shoulders firmly between her elbows, pushing it onto my hair so it sat sheik-like around my head with the tail falling into a cape around my back. 'The boys will want theirs done like that too,' she said.

NELL

We thought our lives would be different, Iris and I. We weren't going to be like Mum doing laundry and sewing to make ends meet. We were going to the technical college to learn to be office girls. Iris got a job first, bookkeeping at Carroll's department store. It suited her because she was so good with figures, and sitting up there in the accounts office, with all that money going out and coming in through the pneumatic chute, she looked like she was in charge. I went to the office at the hospital, typing up letters and reports. If I hadn't married Jack, I would have ended up secretary to the administrator. He told the woman in charge of the office that I had the neatest typing he'd seen, and since he'd come from a big office in Brisbane, he had a high standard to set me against.

Iris started working in 1929 and I was two years behind. It should have only been one year but I lost time at school when Dad died. Mum had to go to work and she needed someone at home to look after Maudie. It was hard to manage a family without a father and we all had to pitch in and do our share. Maudie could have gone to school. It wasn't like she was really sick, but Mum worried about the fits. There was Phyll as well. Someone had to take care of the housework and the washing and be there when Phyll got home from school. I suppose I didn't mind. We didn't in those days. We all helped out. I can't imagine my Kate ever being like that. She likes the good life too much, not to mention her independence.

I went to visit Kate in Sydney once. That girl has a hairdressing bill big enough to feed a family for a week. And as for her wardrobe, she has so many clothes I wouldn't be surprised if she never gets around to wearing some of them. I don't criticise her to her face. I know she's good at heart, but she's become so shallow. Everything is for the image. There's no substance to what she does. She has a good job and she certainly earns enough but it all seems to walk out the door pretty quickly. Jack used to tell me not to worry. 'She's just young. She wants the world,' he would say. Mind you, she had her dad wrapped around her little finger. I wish she'd hurry up and get a bit more settled. She's too easily influenced.

When I worked at the hospital, I thought I was lucky having three outfits to wear to work, and they each lasted me a good eighteen months at least. My favourite was the navy plissé with a wide white collar. It was smart and you could take the collar off to give a different look. That's what we did in those days; we thought of clever ways to make our wardrobes stretch, and Iris and I shared our things to make them stretch even further. Iris had one outfit that I always loved. It had a box-pleated skirt in a cream slub-weave linen and it sat just below the knees. The cotton shirt had a softly rolled collar that tied into a bow at the end of a V-neck. It was simple and feminine and, most of all, it was modern.

We usually made our clothes ourselves. Bought ones were too expensive and Mum did such fine needlework you could hardly see the stitches. She was a tiny woman and always neat; even when things were difficult she always presented herself well. On the hottest summer days her shirt was fresh and held its shape firmly. It was Mum who taught us to sew. On Saturday nights right from when we were young, after the dishes were done and everything cleared away, we gathered around the table in the front room, talking and sewing. Mum preferred simple sewing. 'All that fancy stuff, it's just a waste of time. Give me plain sewing any day. That's how you tell the quality of a girl's work.' Her needle would flash in and out of a piece of white linen or cotton, making buttonholes or stitching a placket. In the early days it might have been a piece of rosebud cotton to make a good dress for one of us. Sometimes she remodelled her old skirts for our clothes and later, while she worked, so did we. Iris and I made samplers from as soon as we could hold a needle without doing ourselves a damage. In 1925 I came second in my age group in the Openings and Fastenings section of the Sewing Exhibition at the Show. I still have the sampler and the certificate in my glory box at home.

After Dad's death the insurance left only a little money, so Mum got some work locally doing laundry and sewing for a bank manager's wife. Mrs Cribb lived in a big place up on Stanton Hill where she was biding her time impatiently until her husband was offered the position he deserved back down south. She spoke incessantly of their life down there and how the north lacked anything of value – fine buildings, shopping, social activities. I don't know how Mum stood it but she persevered until Mrs Chambers from the Criterion Hotel offered her a job as the housekeeper. It was a respectable place, a residential hotel – not just for drinking – and it was a good job for her time.

Dad's death did more than change our circumstances, it changed everything about us. We became a family of women. We had to work harder to make a living, and change our expectations; we had to make things happen for ourselves. Iris was right when she said we had to look out for each other because no one else would.

By the time we were at the technical college, the town was thriving. There were still open paddocks around the suburbs but the main street was a proper town with cafés and specialty stores. All the top entertainment from down south, like The Follies and Sorley's Tent Show, toured the north during the winter. We had a regular train service from Brisbane, and the big shipping companies like Burns Philip and Adelaide Steamships all had offices in town. Imported goods from all over the world were regularly unloaded at the wharves behind the wholesale warehouses along the river. Shipping was so profitable there were even plans to dredge out the river estuary to make a commercial harbour. With mail-order catalogues we could make up the fashions at the same time as all the young women in Sydney or Brisbane and there was a good range of merchandise in the stores. We lacked for nothing. We were as modern as the best of them.

In 1938, when Iris was twenty-five and I was twenty-three, we went to Brisbane for a holiday. It was the first time either of us had been away from the north, and Mum would never have let us go if it hadn't been for the fact that Frances Finney's mother agreed to chaperone half a dozen of us on the trip. We travelled down by train and came back by coastal steamer, sharing two to a cabin on the passenger deck and dining each night with the captain. I bought the smartest pair of cotton gloves and a cloche hat at a department store in George Street and presents for Mum, Maudie and Phyll. I thought I was made. I was spending money I had earned, buying fashion, taking a trip and preparing my trousseau. That's what being a working young Miss meant to me then, having a life and being in charge.

Soon after we got back, we were sitting in the China Lady Tea Room in the main street when Frances's cousin, Jack Cassidy, walked into my life. He pushed his way through the door and stood there for a moment, his hat in his hands, gazing across the room. Then he saw us and his pale blue eyes creased at the edges as his face broke into a smile, and he pulled a chair up to our table.

When Frances introduced us, Jack turned his full gaze on me and said, 'I've seen you at Mass, Ellen. You go to St Mary's, don't you?' I could feel the blush spread upwards and engulf my face. I had seen Jack at Mass every Sunday morning and couldn't believe that he had noticed me. I can't remember what I said in reply, but when we finally stepped out onto the main street I was walking on air.

PHYLL

Maudie and I had very different reasons for liking the house on the south side of town. It was right opposite the church and Maudie went to every Mass. She kept her gloves on a table near the front door so she could whip them on when she heard the bell ring and get across the road in time to sit in the front pew. I had more active interests. The school playground had a set of climbing bars and other children to play with. Mum didn't like me spending my time there. 'I don't want you being a nuisance to the nuns,' she said.

Mum was okay. I could get around her. The problems came from Iris and Nell. They went to technical college and studied office practices so they could find themselves 'positions'. They went to dances and played social tennis and met their friends at the China Lady, or The Metropolitan Tea Rooms in town. Iris subscribed to *Woman's Own* and Nell got *Madam Weigall's Pattern Service* by mail order. They made a new outfit for the Show each year, with gloves, hat, handbag and shoes to match. It didn't suit them to have a little sister who ran wild on the Monkey Island flats.

'You've got to do something about her, Mum,' said Iris, walking through the front door. She hadn't even taken off her jacket. 'It's an embarrassment.' She leaned through the curtained doorway to the bedroom that she shared with

Nell and threw her bag on the bed. 'It's for her own good. She's not a kid any more. She's getting a bad reputation.' Miss Respectable and Miss Reputation! It occurred to me that Iris and Nell were more concerned about what people might think of them than about me.

Nell wasn't as strict as Iris. When Mum had to work and Iris had to finish her education, it was Nell who stayed at home and looked after Maudie and me. I suppose I was more sympathetic towards Nell because she'd had to wait her turn. She could be good fun by herself but when push came to shove she always supported Iris. Those two were lucky. They always had each other. Maudie and I had nothing in common but Mum had this idea that we should be close, the way Iris and Nell were.

'You can go to the dance if Maudie goes too,' she said.

'I'm seventeen, Mum. It's a proper dance. You know Maudie always gets carried away.'

'You aren't going without a chaperone.'

'What if Nell will take me?' I shoved the chair away from the table and tilted back on two legs, waiting for her to answer.

'Nell goes out with Jack on Saturday nights. You can't expect her to be at your beck and call. And Maudie likes the company.'

'She gets embarrassing, Mum. She doesn't know how to make proper conversation. She says silly things and people don't understand.'

'Then I'll go to look out for both of you.'

It wasn't fair that Iris should dictate everything. She could be a real busybody and a bully, too. I wanted to make my own choices but she kept interfering. She talked Mum into sending me to technical college to do bookkeeping, even though she knew I liked being with people. She wanted to shut me up in an office all day with rows and rows of figures. I did well. I was good at figures and I found a job very quickly with Nell in the office at the hospital, but I hated it.

The hospital was run-down and the facilities were unpleasant, for the patients and for the staff, but not long after I started there the new medical superintendent arrived. He was good-looking, young and enthusiastic. According to hospital gossip, he was single-handedly responsible for the increase in trainees and it took a full year for the new nurses to grow out of their crushes on him. He brought lots of new ideas from the big London hospital where he had worked and he and Matron turned the place upside down. They reorganised the nursing and medical sections. They ordered new equipment and drew up plans for upgrading the facilities.

It was a good time for me to start my training. The place fairly buzzed with life. Sister Kenny had opened up her clinic right here in town in 1939 and her polio treatment was being recognised as far away as America. People held nursing in high regard. It was a real profession, not just an office job.

I wanted to wait until I had my new uniform so I could show it off when I told the family my news, but Nell found out and spilled the beans. Iris was furious. 'She'll be in trouble before you know it,' she told Mum. 'With her living in the nurses' quarters, you can't keep an eye on her.'

If only she knew the truth of that. Nursing then was no picnic. Our working week was supposed to be forty-four hours but we did much more than that. We had to turn up half an hour early for our shift to take reports and we had four hours of lectures each week that we had to attend in our own time. Matron and the medical superintendent gave them and they set the end-of-year exams, too, so we didn't dare skip.

On duty we worked like dogs. When I look at what Maudie's nurses do, well, you wouldn't believe the difference! None of our equipment was disposable. We had to sterilise all the syringes and the catheters and needles. There were only a couple of domestics for the whole hospital, so the nurses also swept and mopped the floors and washed the dishes and cleaned the bathrooms and toilets. We even washed the dirty linen by hand, before we sent it to the laundry. And that wasn't the end of it. More than once I helped the wardsman carry stretcher cases up the stairs. I guarantee the only time I sat down was at the end of a shift when we had to make up the dressings for the next day's use, and by then we were too tired to speak.

From her flat on the ground floor Matron kept a tight

leash on the nurses' quarters so there was not much chance of hanky-panky. The duty sister did a bed check of the nurses after lights out at eleven o'clock, though there was hardly any need since we were always so exhausted we were snoring our heads off the minute they hit the pillow. The home was badly run-down. It was a wooden building with creaky casements and peeling paint work, and even if you wanted to sneak out, there's no way you could have done it. You couldn't even walk to the toilet during the night without waking every soul in the place.

When the war started, the action was so far away that it didn't really touch us at first. We followed the news on the radio, listening to reports of German advances through places we only knew from geography lessons. The closest it came to home was when the local council called a special sitting to change the name of one of the suburbs from German Gardens to Belgian Gardens. They had done it once before, during the First World War, but afterwards, with high hopes and good faith, they had changed it back. This time I didn't think the Germans would get another chance. Local boys joined up and went off to fight. Esme O'Connor's mother got a telegram saying Esme's brother was killed in a training accident and Mrs O'Connor, whose family had been Fenians, thanked the Lord for answering her prayer not to let him die fighting on the side of the British.

Nell's wedding to Jack Cassidy was in November

1941 and I was bridesmaid. I finally felt as if my family was proud of me. Nell bought the pea-green geisha silk for my dress, along with the satin for her wedding dress, just after she got engaged. It was lucky that she always planned ahead because when the war brought a fabric shortage, you needed coupons to buy cloth, and the stuff that used to come from Japan you just couldn't get any more.

NELL

Jack and I had a lovely day for our wedding. We were married at St Francis's, across the road from Mum's. Iris was carrying her first at the time and it wasn't appropriate for her to be my matron of honour, so Phyll was my bridesmaid instead. She looked a picture of prettiness in that dress. The colour brought out her lovely green eyes. Looking at her, you'd never believe what a tomboy she'd been. Jack's mother made the bridesmaid's hat with net and flowers to match the dress and she did the bouquets, too. Mine was made of lily-of-the-valley and gypsophila loosely bound with satin ribbon, and Phyll's was threaded with the spotted net that lined her hat.

Jack's parents had a big house with the living areas opening onto a wide enclosed verandah where we had the wedding breakfast. Mrs Cassidy did all the catering herself. I wondered how on earth I would ever meet her expectations. Of course none of us expected that within a month we would have a war in the Pacific that would come right to our very own doorstep.

It was 6 December 1941. Jack and I heard the news on the station platform in Brisbane. We were starting the second leg of our honeymoon, taking the train down to Sydney. Jack changed the tickets and we came straight home. Our soldiers were already in Europe fighting for the British. There was no one left to protect our homes. We were terrified. The army was calling up men who had never handled a rifle and didn't know which end to shoot out of. Here we were, barely married, and it looked like Jack would be sent off to fight in terrible conditions in some tropical jungle.

In 1941 the town population was thirty-five thousand. The war brought a troop invasion and the town swelled to four times its size. All this activity made our busy provincial life seem sleepy and completely overwhelmed us. Civilian buildings were taken over for military use and for housing servicemen, air bases and military installations were under construction, and encampments sprang up on vacant land all over the place for the troops on their way to the fighting. From one day to the next the whole landscape could change, and the voices around would sound so strange. It was frightening.

We gathered around the radio to hear the news of the Japanese advance through Asia. Each day they came closer and closer to us, and names like Borneo, Mindanao and the Solomons became so familiar we spoke about them as if we had been there ourselves. When Bill joined up and was sent to New Guinea, Iris took her baby, Neville, back home to live with Mum and Maudie. Luckily Phyll was at the nurses' home or there wouldn't have been room. Then Jack and his brother both joined up and I moved in with his parents, who lived a few blocks away from Mum. We only went out when necessary and rarely did we venture into town. It was far too dangerous with all those foreign servicemen about. Jack's dad was in the Special Reserve on account of his work in the Railway and he was out night after night, leaving Mrs Cassidy and me by ourselves in that big house. We were terrified. The paper had daily reports of disturbances and often there were shootings and stabbings. It was nothing to hear drunken soldiers shouting at each other and fighting as they went past in the street late at night and some of those Americans were so black you couldn't see them in the dark. There was a lot of bootleg liquor about, and many of the men were armed.

One morning a dead body was found on the steps of the post office. It was a soldier who had come off worst in an argument where weapons got involved. For years after that it seemed like you could see the mark on the steps where the blood had seeped into the stonework and left its stain.

PHYLL

There were eighty of us nurses at the hospital and we must have cared for well over two hundred people a day. That included the troops, until each of the services set up their own hospitals. We stretched our shifts to cover the work. I was up at five every morning and on the job by six. There was nothing glamorous about boiling eggs for the patients' breakfasts and washing the dishes after supper. When my shift finished I still had classes. Despite all that, I loved it. Dealing with people suited my nature and we were doing an important job at a time when our country needed us. It was real nursing, not like those social butterflies down south who volunteered for the Red Cross.

Our uniforms were royal blue with a wide white collar and white cuffs on the short sleeves, and we had different caps to mark the year we had reached in training. The seamstress at the hospital made them. I always wore mine when I came home. It seemed to declare the importance of my role in this war and offset some of Iris's criticisms.

Iris and Nell spent a lot of time sitting around Mum's kitchen table, the way they used to when they embroidered doilies for their glory boxes before they were married. Now they knitted matinee jackets and bootees and Iris remade Bill's old suit as trousers for Neville to grow into. Nell and Iris were lucky. They had always had each other for company.

It was quiet over on the south side compared to the hospital. The troops didn't move much in those residential areas but exaggerations and rumours did. People had heard stories about the camp followers and the local prostitutes and assumed it meant everyone. The nurses especially got a bad name just because we were in close contact with them at the hospital. Bill wrote to Iris that the servicemen in New Guinea knew the Yanks were getting all the women back home. You couldn't wear a pair of stockings without being accused of going with the Americans.

It was impossible to keep all my comings and goings a secret. I went home each week for my day off, so the family knew when I went to parties and dances and they knew who I was with. I wasn't going to sneak around trying to hide, especially since I wasn't doing anything wrong. Mum knew that. There were dances and the pictures and no shortage of escorts keen to take a girl out and have a good time. I worked hard and the men we met were always nice. Why shouldn't I have enjoyed myself? I had little enough time to do it and who knew when this war would end – or how? Iris and Nell had their husbands and their families and their lives and their overactive imaginations. People my age hadn't even started to live when the war broke out and we didn't know if we would ever see the other side of it. It was no wonder we tried to pack as much fun into the time we had.

Nurses were on call twenty-four hours a day, and in case of an air raid we had to report back to hospital immediately to help move patients to the shelter that was built in the basement of the maternity ward. The ones who couldn't be moved we left on mattresses under their beds, with extra mattresses piled up on each side of them. We gave them a bottle of water and ran for our lives to the shelter. It was all very primitive but we did our best. Heaven knows what would have happened to them if the hospital had ever been hit. Luckily the worst damage was a few broken windows from the over-enthusiastic anti-air-raid gunners who were supposed to be protecting us from the hill opposite the hospital.

The Japs bombed the harbour twice in July. Nell's pregnancy was showing by then and Jack's father organised for her to be evacuated south to his brother's farm. Iris and Neville stayed on with Mum and Maudie. Iris had the back room and Maudie slept in the double bed with Mum. When I stayed over I bunked down on the day bed in the living room so I could come in late without disturbing anyone.

The Battle of the Coral Sea turned things around. Our boys started to drive the Japs back and the auxiliary hospitals in schools around town weren't needed any more. For a time things eased up in the hospital. There were fewer soldiers needing treatment and our wards could take more civilian patients. Then the dengue fever epidemic took hold and we were run off our feet all over again. It seemed as if every time we learnt to cope with one emergency, another sprang up to test us.

Despite the medical superintendent's hard work, the war put a stop to the maintenance work on the hospital buildings, and conditions were worse than when I started my training. They were desperate for staff and the government was desperate for money to keep the war effort going. It even looked as if Maudie would lose the pension because they didn't count her fits as an obvious disability.

By the end of my second year, the nurses' home was in a terrible state, especially in the winter. People think that winters never get cold in the tropics, but we were near the sea and at night, when the wind was up, it blew through the cracks in the wall of the house and the loose sash windows rattled mercilessly in their frames. The blankets they supplied were so thin we resorted to bringing our own and there was such a shortage of cutlery that we had to take it in turns to eat.

It was sad to see all the buildings getting so run-down, especially the nurses' home. Once it was a rather grand house for these parts, sitting at the top of an elegant drive that led up through the terraced hospital grounds, past the various wards, outbuildings and the medical superintendent's residence. The drive was lined with mango and black bean trees, and underneath the branches the garden beds were thick with agapanthus. It took maybe ten minutes to walk from the lower buildings all the way around the drive to the house, but we nurses used to cut across the gardens and climb up the terraces to get there faster. We thought nothing of doing it alone and at all hours, until Ellen Casey saw the prowler.

People were divided over Ellen's story. One camp said she was tired; she'd worked extra shifts that week and she must have imagined the shadowy figure cowering in the garden near the ablutions block. That building was so run-down there were holes in the walls large enough to poke a fist through. Ellen said she got such a fright when she saw the dark shape duck and scuttle away that she stood rooted to the spot, screaming loudly. The girls who were showering grabbed their towels and dressing gowns and rushed out to see what the commotion was. Matron and Duty Sister came running with lamps but there was no sign of a peeping Tom. The next day the groundsman was put to work patching up the wall of the showers and everyone thanked Ellen for finding a way to get it fixed.

Some of the nurses called for more security, especially late at night, but the others howled them down. Matron said to keep the matter under our hats. The town was already flooded with rumours of 'loose nurses'; we didn't want to add to them, and if there wasn't a prowler already, we didn't want to encourage one.

No one argued with Matron but amongst ourselves we kept talking about it. We were all used to dealing with cheeky men since there were plenty of them in the wards, but being watched in our rooms was another matter. Ellen was sure she had seen someone, so we kept an eye out for signs. Occasionally we found plants flattened in the garden right next to the slats outside the ground-floor dormitory. It was always on the side away from the drive and where the spreading branches of a black bean tree threw a deep shadow. One night Mary Harvey was saying prayers by the side of her bed when she raised her head and looked straight into a set of eyes that were staring back at her. She couldn't tell anything about the face but she swore it was real. Matron called us all together in the dining room and gave us a lecture about excitable behaviour and letting our imaginations run away with us. For peace of mind we decided to walk in pairs or groups at night, and the hospital found a supply of torches so we wouldn't be completely in the dark.

You could never rely on Dot McCarthy to keep her word. She either forgot or kept her promise badly. I was already in strife with Sister for being late on duty after my day off. Then, on top of my regular ward duties, she ordered me to prepare all the dressings for the next shift while the other nurses were on tea break. I asked Dot to bring me back something because I hadn't eaten since breakfast and I knew that by the time I got to the dining room what was left of the food would be cold. Of course she forgot, but she offered to finish winding the bandages while I raced over to get a meal. There was corned beef, cabbage, and onions in white sauce. The tail end of the cabbage was swimming in salty water, the white sauce had gone hard and the last piece of meat was mostly cold fat.

I felt queasy through the rest of my shift, especially when I was asked to dress a badly infected leg. My stomach turned and I had to race to the laundry room to splash water on my face. When I came back, Sister was standing over the bandage box.

'Nurse Minton!' Her voice thundered through the ward. I looked down at my uniform to see if it was clean. When I raised my eyes, she was holding up a bandage that was completely unlike the neat rolls we were expected to make. This one had been wound so roughly it was misshapen, with pieces of bandage sticking out. I looked in the box. The last ones done were the same. I looked across at Dot. She bent over a patient, busying herself with something to avoid my eye.

'You don't finish your shift until each and every bandage is rolled properly and the dressings cupboard is in perfect order from top to bottom.'

I groaned silently. It would be nearly midnight by the

time I got to bed. My stomach did another heave and I had to shut my mouth tightly.

When I stepped outside, the air was thick with the scent of rotting mangoes and I could hear the small noises of possums feasting on ripe fruit in the nearby trees. The humidity sat heavily on my shoulders but, a short distance away, waves smashed onto the beach and the sound carried through the still night and gave it a sense of freshness after the dragging heat of the day.

It was only when my foot slipped and I stumbled forward onto my hands and knees that I realised I had automatically turned off the drive and onto the track through the garden. It was dark and I didn't have a torch, but since I knew the track well I decided to struggle on. It would get me home faster. I was angry that Dot had let me down and I was angry at the way she did it, leaving me in the ward sister's bad books.

He thumped me so hard in the back the pressure forced me up against a wall. I couldn't breathe. My head spun. Something sharp cut into my cheek. Then I was flying and a sickening thud ran through me as I landed on my back. He planted the full force of his knee in my stomach and pinned me to the ground. I punched and scratched. His hand smothered my face with the scent of tobacco. I imagined his fingers leaving brown stains all over me as he ripped and grabbed and pulled at me. His hands were everywhere at once. My thighs burnt as his knee forced me apart and I felt a sudden sharp pain that sent the bitter taste of vomit spilling from my mouth. A loud slap wrenched my face sideways. 'Stupid bitch,' he said, and I felt his spit on my face.

KATE

It only takes a second to move from panic to relief.

I wake suddenly. The alarm hasn't gone off. Within a second I collapse back onto the pillow as I realise it's Saturday. I don't want to go anywhere. I want to stay in my pyjamas all day.

There are noises coming from the kitchen. Voices. Dan must have the radio on. I lie in bed, eyes closed, thinking of all the things I need to do. One after another they tumble through my mind, and cutting irresistibly across them is the idea of breakfast in bed and a long lie-in.

'Katey.' Dan's voice thunders down the hall.

I mumble a reply in the hope that he'll leave the tray on the floor beside me.

'Katey. Are you awake?' He's in the room.

'If I wasn't before, I would be now,' I mumble.

He lands enthusiastically on the bed. 'Come on. Get up. We're meeting Steve and Clare for brunch.'

My whole body sags into the bed. I not only have to get up and get dressed, I also have to be sociable.'You mean Steve and Clare with the torturous toddlers and the screaming baby, don't you? You really know how to ruin my weekend.' I know full well that brunch will end up at dinner with pizzas and kids at Clare and Steve's place. The whole day will go by leaving me feeling washed out and used up in its wake.

Dan and I rarely argue and we never have grubby fights or squabbles. Clare calls us the Immaculatas. She and Stephen are always at each other, playing out their petty quarrels and spats against a chorus of squalling, crawling kids. Dan and I stand there on the sidelines, just the two of us, in silence. We don't have disagreements, just differences of opinion, and we prefer to keep them private.

'Come on, Katey. You love the kids.'

'Love the kids? Sometimes, Dan, you can get it so wrong!'

It took a long time for us to talk about having kids. We got along well. We had fun. There wasn't any pressure to extend ourselves. Dan comes from a big family with lots of nieces and nephews, and my brothers have enough between them to keep Mum happy. In my mind, babies would just come along when we were ready. I never considered not having them. I just went looking for a simple answer to the simple question, Why do I hurt? A sharp-tongued specialist snatched away the choice and left me with the hard-edged clicking of her heels on the hospital linoleum.

Talking about children changes the way you see each other. You stop being playmates. Suddenly you're organisers, managers, planners – parents. Each time Clare was pregnant, Stephen trotted out his old joke about human beings incubating for nine months to give parents time to get used to the idea. With in-vitro you don't get nine months. You don't even get one. From the first day of treatment you have to be absolutely certain that this baby is what you want most in the world. When you're asking for a miracle, you can't risk faltering in your determination. Even one small stumble might jinx your chance. You learn to hold your breath, as if holding your hopes inside. You learn to be prepared to do whatever is necessary to make it happen. You stop being a couple and become part of a team where everyone knows when you have sex, how often, what your cycle is, when you ovulate. You're completely exposed.

Dan puts out a hand and strokes my arm. 'Sorry, love, but I honestly thought that after yesterday you could do with some cheerful company.'

'Thanks,' I say, with a voice as flat as my feelings. Yesterday they told us we had failed again. 'I could have done without the reminder.'

Dan's face falls and he looks as sombre as I feel.

'I just . . . You could have asked me first, about the brunch.' I want to add, You should have thought of me as a separate person, not some attachment of yours, automatically compelled to do whatever you might decide. Instead I say, 'And what about househunting? We are supposed to be looking for a place of our own, aren't we?'

'Katey, couldn't we just have a bit of fun today?'

Listening to Clare carry on about the trials of being a mother isn't my idea of fun. Looking at her cuddling her babies and complaining about how much effort they take, I want to scream at her: It's not fair, you got them so easily, you don't deserve them.

Dan gets up and heads for the shower. That's the way he does things. He likes them to be straightforward, no discussion. He can't see the point of going through the ins and outs and dissecting how you feel. You either do it or you don't. He doesn't waste time befuddled by emotions.

All of a sudden I need to cry and I lie against the pillows wishing he would come back and cuddle me, but I know that in ten minutes I'll be calling him irresponsible or unreliable or inconsiderate. That's how it is these days, swinging from one side to the other until I don't know how I feel, until I wish I could swing right off the planet.

GAYLE

It's the trees that make this place – shade trees with lush, leafy foliage and trees with a profusion of flowers. They are what save us from the dull brown sameness of the bush. Across the city and around the barren base of the Hill, poincianas, banyan figs, umbrella trees and coconut palms all lend colour and shade to break the ordinariness of the town. Imports from every corner of the earth, immigrants like us, gathered from everywhere and put down here in the hope that they too will find nourishment and spread roots.

Because we live in the tropics, southerners imagine this place to be full of lush rainforests running down to the reef. They don't understand how it can be humid and dry at the same time, how the earth can be parched when moisture hangs in the air and how the country can be so desiccated when we are next to the sea. They can't imagine what it's like to live here, and when I stand back and take stock of it I can't describe it either. The daily minutiae glide by. What needs to be done we do without consideration. I suppose that's the way you forge a life, one step after another, one minute at a time. The big picture only appears when you have gone far enough to look back and see it. When we have visitors, I take them to the lookout at the top of Castle Hill. Looking inland from that craggy rock face, toward the mountain range, you can see the line of deep green from the river as it curves across the flat brown plain, where a grid of roads and streets and rows and rows of silver roofs mark out the endless suburbs. From up here the gardens and parks appear as no more than scraggly patches of colour melding into the background. On a clear day, when you turn your back on the plain and gaze seaward, the view takes in the beaches and the bay, across the container ships in the channel to the Island and beyond. The only thing you can smell is the freshness of the sea air and the only sound is the wind as it whistles around the rocky face.

From a plane the faded ground so far below shows up like an X-ray photograph, intersected by broad rivers that snake around the flat coastal plain in exaggerated bends and curves. The only evidence of vegetation is the line of green where the washed out floodplains meet the sea, the line where the mangroves grow. From the sea newcomers are easily deceived by the appearance of lush vegetation hugging a firm coastline, never suspecting the stinking muddy bed beneath that glossy green line.

Nowadays the distinctive blue blush of jacarandas appears in clouds around the older suburbs each September. The white cedar comes out in November with a floral shower of delicate mauve and white. In summer there's the vivid orange of African tulips. All year round Blue Mountain parrots feed off the large cupped flowers of the native kapok tree, and bougainvillea spills dramatically in remarkable shades of fuchsia and crimson, deep purple and white down the cliffs overlooking the Strand. Without them all the city would be barren and uninviting, no more than a salty river plain with the bold and barren rock face of the Hill gazing seaward.

Lately I have been building a garden, a lush oasis around the double-brick house that was Doug's home when I moved into it. We've worked on the garden together, as if laying the foundations for our new life. Doug tackled the heavy work with that endless enthusiasm of his and I stepped back and planned the layout and selected the plants. The garden already had some thick-leaved anthuriums and an established grove of banana trees, heavy with deep purple fruit, but I wanted masses of luxuriant foliage, with as many types of exotic, colourful and lush plants as I could find, like lianas and aloes and waterlilies floating in a pool. I wanted a refuge where I could work quietly away at my drawing, sheltered from the dryness and the heat of the plain. There's an open patio where I sit to work and already the clusters of ferns that I transplanted from my old house overflow from their pots and the air is cooled by the constant moisture of the leaf mould.

I took a commission recently to do the illustrations for a series of children's books based on local stories, and the wildlife that comes in to share my garden has already found its way into the drawings. Every morning from my desk on the patio I watch a gecko emerge just as the sun is beginning to rise over the roof line. He comes out from the base of the banana trees, scampers across the lawn to drink at the pool. Then he scampers back to a broad flat rock where he can sun himself and still dart for cover should danger lurk by. Doug called him Horace. I argued with him: 'That's an irreverent name for such an exotic creature.'

But Horace it stays.

KATE

The airport sign proudly announces 'Gateway to the Golden North'. We disembark via stairs to the runway, descending into the suffocatingly humid heat that smothers my enthusiasm each time I arrive. The long-sleeved cotton shirt that seemed inadequate in the fresh Sydney morning now clings to my sticky skin as I walk across the tarmac. Apart from a few light aircraft offering joy flights over the reef, ours is the only plane in sight.

Uncle Vic is there to meet me. He gives me a peck on the cheek and guides me briskly to the luggage collection. The families returning from holidays and the army personnel on transfer who shared my flight already surround the carousel. Uncle Vic stretches on tiptoes and rocks from side to side in an effort to see the luggage as it emerges on the conveyor belt. I look at the coffee shop and wonder whether it's worth taking a risk on a flat white. I'm a three-cups-a-day girl. It's my only drug of addiction and so far today I haven't scored one. I'm wary because previous experience has taught me that good coffee is a rare find north of Noosa.

'What are your suitcases like, love?'

Small, smart and black like my mood, I think to myself. It's eleven-thirty in the morning. I've travelled three thousand kilometres. I haven't had my morning dose of caffeine and I'm tired. I shake the irritation out of my voice and give him my best and brightest PR smile. 'There's one,' I say, pointing, and Uncle Vic darts through the crowd in time to retrieve the travel case.

'How's the fishing these days, Uncle Vic?' He used to be a keen fisherman. At one time he was a champion angler. His fishing trophies are displayed around his living room and there are photos of him with one prize catch after another. The trophies all sport silver-plated fish balancing on wooden stands with small plaques to identify the year and the competition. Auntie Phyll once said she wished he'd take up bowls instead because bowlers smelt better than fishermen and they got useful tournament prizes like cake platters and crystal salad bowls.

'I've given it away, love,' says Vic, bending down slightly to peer through the huddle of people. 'There's too much of it these days. All those Taiwanese trawlers we see on the news. There'll be nothing left for the world to eat in a few years.' Suddenly he ducks between the elbows of a couple of hefty army types and reappears clutching an overnighter that is the perfect match to my travel case. He holds it aloft like a prize red emperor. The grin that spreads across his face reveals a perfectly even set of dentures.

'That it?' he asks.

'You're a champ, Uncle Vic.'

I have to skip a step to catch up with him as he speeds out to the car, his bandy legs moving so fast that his short body rocks from side to side with the weight of my bags. By the time I reach the car, he has the bags stowed away in the boot and the passenger door unlocked. He starts the engine as I settle into my seat, and before I can clip the seatbelt into place he pulls out of the parking bay.

'Traffic clogs up at the exit if everyone's trying to leave at once,' he says.

I cast a glance around the parking lot. There are maybe forty vehicles, including the taxis and a commuter bus. I think of the peak-hour traffic that Dan negotiated as he drove me to the airport this morning. Cool, calm Dan. I suddenly wish I could see him tonight. I want to share every detail of my day so I can pack all the bits neatly within the parameters of normal. I've only just arrived here and already I crave the familiarity of life with Dan – going to work, coming home, watching telly, a video, eating spinach pizza from the Lebanese round the corner, reading in bed.

This place that I once thought of as ordinary now seems foreign to me.

The airport is out along the main highway north, next to the Town Common and near the mudflats. The new town spreads away from them, all the way to the foothills of Mount Louisa. Out there the river gets wider and deeper and on each side is the sprawl of air-conditioned brick houses, perfectly even front lawns, shopping malls and taverns. When we get to Ingham Road, Vic casts barely a glance in that direction before turning left toward the old town and the old suburb where he and Auntie Phyll live within a sandfly's bite of the mangroves.

Ingham Road is a long, straight stretch of road through to the Causeway but Vic doesn't go above thirty, travelling in the left-hand lane. This used to be a two-lane highway, built up above the level of the mudflat to minimise the flooding that came regularly each January with the combination of the king tides and the Wet. It still has sections of concrete slab because the flooding invariably rose higher than the engineers expected and washed away sections of the road.

Vic drives his manual car with one foot sitting lightly on the clutch. We grind to a halt at the traffic lights on the corner of Kings Road. The six-lane highway is black with an inky newness. It's the middle of the day, there's only light traffic around, but as the lights turn green Vic takes off with a cautious slowness that makes the driver behind toot his horn.

'Impatient fool,' says Vic gruffly. 'It's his sort that cause accidents.'

'How's the family?' I ask, to take my mind off the frustratingly slow drive into town.

'They're good, thanks love,' says Vic, firming his grip on the steering wheel.

'Mum said Peter's moved to South Australia.'

'He's a corporal now. Bryan's managing the motor repair shop. Brendan is selling spare parts at the Holden dealership. He's a collar-and-tie man now and Paul's a phys-ed teacher at the high school out at Mount Louisa.'

I only know Mount Louisa as the outline I used to study on the horizon. On Sunday mornings after church, Dad took Mum for driving lessons on the old wartime airstrips right out of town and as we drove up and down and up and down the crumbling tarmac, I used to stare out at the mountain line in the distance. It was covered with sparse bush and if you looked carefully enough you could make out individual trees silhouetted against the lightness of the sky. Now it's one of the new suburbs that sprawl out to the west of the city. To me, it's just a place name but I can picture the rawness of the new brick-and-concrete school buildings and the houses and the gardens that will flourish one day if they get enough water and attention. Up and down the coast, they're always the same.

'He and Natalie have built a new house at Wulguru. They're expecting another baby in July. That'll make three for them. Brendan and Bryan have both got three already in high school and Peter has four.'

'So you and Auntie Phyll have enough grandkids to keep you busy,' I suggest.

'Oh no!' Uncle Vic's reply is tight. 'The boys never expected us to be at their beck and call for babysitting and the like.' I stifle a sigh and try to think of another course of conversation. This is promising to be a long haul.

'How are Mum and Auntie Iris bearing up?'

'Coping, love, coping,' says Uncle Vic. 'Mind you, Phyll has been a tower of strength. Going backwards and forwards to the hospital and taking care of all the washing and other business that needs to be done.' He keeps his eyes well focused on the road as he speaks. 'Not that she minds, of course. We're only too happy to pitch in and do our share.'

'What about Gayle?' She's a stalwart. She would have been there to help out but, more importantly, Uncle Vic might fill in the gaps that Mum left open.

'She's a good girl, young Gayle,' says Uncle Vic, quietly ignoring the fact that, at fifty-five, Gayle is already a grandmother. 'You know, she's left Noel and taken up with some new fella.' He looks in the rear-vision mirror and frowns. We're approaching the Causeway and he has to cross three lanes of traffic to be in the right turning lane. I wait, knowing he can't speak. The green arrow comes on just as we reach the intersection and he swings the car stiffly around, then immediately turns left and we're into familiar territory. His shoulders settle down and he wipes a sweaty palm against his shorts.

'His name's Doug something or other. We haven't met him at all but he's certainly been about.'

'What happened?'

'Blest if I know.'

Gayle was twenty-three years old when she married Noel Keary, a good Catholic boy from a good Catholic family that Auntie Iris and Uncle Bill knew well. Noel finished his accountancy exams while Gayle had three babies – all boys – and stayed at home to raise them in those suburbs we'd seen in the distance.

'Did she say why she did it?'

'Not to us, she didn't. Apparently she just packed up her things while Noel was at work and left the bags inside the front door. He comes home to find two large suitcases with clothes in them and a note saying she's collecting them all on Saturday morning. It was the day after Maudie took sick. Noel's pretty cut up about it but she looks like she's got a new lease on life!'

Gayle, gorgeous Gayle of the elegant A-line dresses and stiletto heels. For years she's done the right thing by everybody else, maybe now she's doing something for herself.

Uncle Vic and Auntie Phyll live in an old Queenslander on the south side, near the mangroves and close enough to the container terminals to hear the ships being loaded and unloaded through the night. It's a high-blocked house with big verandahs and wooden louvres and an under-the-house with cement floors, old furniture and lots of pot plants. Everyone around here has an under-the-house, unless they live in a low-blocked house in which case they have an out-the-back. High-blocked houses are traditional in the north because of the floods and the heat. Their advantage in floods is obvious but their benefits in the heat only become apparent if you've lived through the stiflingly muggy weather of the Wet. The higher you are at night, the more airflow there is, so it's more comfortable to sleep upstairs with the windows open. Nowadays even the old houses have been fitted with insect screens but when I was a child we used mosquito nets and coils in the worst part of summer. I remember waking up in the darkness, swinging in the slack where the mosquito net was tucked under the mattress. How many times must it have caught me like that as I rolled out of bed in my sleep?

You really appreciate an under-the-house on the hottest of summer days. It's more protected from the sun and stays cooler, especially if you hose down the cement floors. During the rainy season, I used to lie in the dry open space under our house with my face inches from the downpour, watching the heavy monsoonal drops carve dips in the sandy spots in the garden.

Mum and Auntie Phyll are sitting under the house

when Uncle Vic pulls into the driveway. They hear the crunch of the car tyres against sand and come out to greet us. Auntie Phyll looks just the same as always, with a broad grin and permed hair all frizzy at the ends, but Mum is different. She is smaller and more bent over than the last time I saw her and she walks very slowly, holding onto a wall or a chair back or something similar for reassurance. These are the changes I miss when we talk by phone. I always feel as if she is close by in my life, sometimes too close, but the telephone lines that keep us in touch don't disclose the shrinking of her body and the curving of her spine.

She thrusts two spindly arms around me and hugs me tight, barely reaching my shoulders where once she met me eye to eye. She is so pleased to see me, I have to swallow hard at the lump in my throat that threatens to choke me. I hug her back and hold my breath in an effort to gag the tears before they well up and spill over. I've spent all these years running off and building my life so I could feel free of her expectations and demands, and her revenge has been to grow white-haired and elderly behind my back. If I had been here, living here and seeing her daily, those signs of her ageing would have crept into my consciousness little by little instead of striking me with a loaded punch. It's more than just my absence. My mother is forty-four years older than I am. She is my closest relative, already grey-haired before I reached adulthood. Her ageing wields a greater power over me because I have always seen her as old but physically strong and capable. I see myself reflected in her loneliness and frailty and I feel guilt at being an absent daughter.

Vic takes my bags upstairs while Auntie Phyll and Mum usher me in under the house.

Mum's rosary beads are nestled in the swag of the squatter's chair. 'Were you praying my plane would fall out of the sky?' I ask. Her mouth screws into a smile and she quickly scoops the beads up into her pocket. 'You know jolly well I wasn't.' She doesn't want to admit that the whole time she was talking with Phyll her fingers were automatically counting off the beads and under her breath she was dedicating decades of the rosary to the patron saint of air travel. That's the suffocating solicitude that I escaped from. At a distance, I can accept her praying for me so intensely and in my moments of crisis I have been happy that she did.

'Would you like a cup of coffee?' offers Auntie Phyll.

'You should be drinking tea.' Uncle Vic steps off the last of the back steps and into the shade under the house. 'There's antioxidants in it. They're good for you.'

'Him and his blessed antioxidants,' Auntie Phyll hisses at me as Uncle Vic saunters across the cool cement.

'Stop your complaining, Phyll O'Riordan, you even sound like an old woman.'

'I'll give you old woman,' says Auntie Phyll, leaving me

suspicious that she might not be altogether amused. 'All day and all night, your brain is full of those vitamin and mineral supplements.'

'Well, you have to admit he looks the picture of health.' Mum gives a little laugh to lighten the atmosphere.

Auntie Phyll bristles slightly and I take the opportunity to interrupt. 'A cold drink would go down well, thanks Auntie Phyll.'

Uncle Vic wanders out to the sprinkler that's watering his ferns. Phyll slips on her house shoes and walks over to the steps, her soles scraping against the cement with each step. Mum doesn't make any move to rise. She leaves Phyll to manage on her own. I am here and she wants to savour the time with me.

'How was the flight?' asks Mum. This is how we usually start, skirting around each other, discussing generalities. I know she'd be happy to hear me talk about anything. She's thrilled that I've come. For a few hours her pleasure will make the trip worthwhile.

The canvas seat of the squatter's chair is slung like a deck chair. With nothing to support her body in an upright position, Mum has slid down into the swag of the seat and sits almost curled up. Her long, slender legs are now thin and bony. She makes me think of a newborn foal, all arms and legs and knees, folding and unfolding in its attempts to stand. 'What about Maudie?' There's really no news. Her condition was stabilised days ago and now it is just a matter of waiting. The stroke was severe. The doctors doubt she will recover. And what would she recover to? It's been years since she recognised her sisters and eighteen months since she spoke her last word. Day after day she lies in her room in the nursing home, turned and fed and bathed and toileted by the staff.

'She's been well looked after,' says Mum. Her words flow out as a well-rehearsed story.

'Uncle Vic says Gayle has a new boyfriend,' I interrupt.

'Uncle Vic shouldn't gossip.' She tries to suppress a smile but only succeeds in making it look naughty.

'Well?' I persist.

'Well what?' she replies.

Now I know there's something to tell. 'Who is he? What's he like?'

'Didn't I teach you anything? Don't you know it's a sin to talk about people behind their backs?'

'So you haven't met him but Auntie Iris has told you all about him.'

'I'm not saying anything. You can ask her yourself. We'll see Gayle and Iris at the nursing home this afternoon.'

My shirt sticks to my skin. The sweat collects under the cups of my bra and a rash is starting where the underwire rubs against my damp skin. I long to wash the stickiness away.

'Would you like to have a shower before lunch?' Mum reads my thoughts. 'We'd better make a move if you want to freshen up. Phyll will have lunch nearly ready.' She grabs the bottom rung of the chair to haul herself out. I stretch out a hand to help her but she's a dead weight, using her arms to pull because there's no muscle strength in her body.

'You need to do some exercise.'

'I'm flat out getting through the day as it is.'

She walks across the cement with slow small steps, unsure of keeping her balance if she widens her stride. At the back stairs, she holds onto the railing with both hands to pull herself upwards. Her middle has spread into a round ball without muscle but the rest of her, her shoulders and upper arms, have all shrunk away. She climbs the stairs slowly, pulling from her forearms and pushing from her feet in a way that propels her body upwards with a jerky motion. I put my hand on the small of her back and press gently, frightened she might lose the momentum and topple backwards.

'Watch it,' she says. 'You'll push me over.'

I release the pressure a little but keep my hand there to make me feel more secure with her balance. 'You need one of those escalator chairs,' I tease.

'I would if I lived in a high-blocked house. I couldn't do this more than once a day.'

I wonder how she manages the downward trip, standing on the top landing and looking at the distance to the ground. I can see her holding onto the side with both hands and gingerly taking one step at a time. 'No,' she says, guessing my thoughts. 'I come down backwards, so I won't see anything if I fall.'

I'm suddenly very glad she lives in a low-blocked house.

Uncle Vic has set my bags at the foot of the bed in the room that Mum and I are to share. I rummage through them in search of something light and comfortable to change into and some talc to dry out the rash.

The bathroom mirror reflects a person I'm not sure I want to be familiar with. She looks like me but my face has grown thinner of late. The plumpness has fallen away, leaving me looking more like my mother. My belly has never been flat. It makes a soft mound under my skirt and if I raise myself on tiptoes I can see its naked roundness. My hips are carrying the beginnings of a spare tyre. Mum always used to say, 'You can't fatten thoroughbreds,' and I wonder if I too am a thoroughbred.

Maudie's room at the nursing home is bare. The linoleum-tiled floor glows with a hospital-like cleanness and its unlined brick walls remind me of a highway motel room. The venetian blind gives a suggestion of privacy but does nothing to soften the bluntness of the room with its built-in cupboard, bedside cabinet, hospital-style bed and an easychair where Auntie Iris sits. Mum is next to her on a plastic garden chair that Gayle carried in from the veran-dah so that together they can oversee us packing Maudie's things. Everyone agrees that she will not return here from hospital.

'She didn't have a lot in the end,' says Mum.

'She didn't need it,' says Auntie Iris.

'Not like when she was at home,' says Mum. 'You couldn't close the wardrobe door, she had that many clothes.'

'I don't think she ever wore some of them,' says Auntie Iris. 'It was a real waste.'

'Well, that's the way she was.'

We have been through this before. We sorted through Nana's things when she died and through Maudie's when they sold the house and moved her into the nursing home. This time feels different. In Nana's house there were boxes of sepia photos and bits and pieces left over from so many people's lives. It took us a day just to sort through them. This time there is no excitement of discovery or connection with the past. There are no photos, no books and no ornaments. A metal tray empty of medicines sits on the bedside cabinet and the cupboard is neatly stacked with unused clothes and the few personal items that she was allowed to bring to the home. In the end, she was a commodity, the stuff of business for this place. Patient no. 306, stroke, social security no. 17598, aged pension. They cared for her well but amongst all of these things there is no trace of the sad, eccentric person we made fun of when we were kids.

'That hug-me-tight.' Auntie Iris points to the knitted bedjacket in my hands. 'That's a pretty shade of apricot. Where did it come from?'

'Phyll gave it to her last birthday but it's never been worn,' says Mum. 'We could send it over to Robbie O'Dowd. She often came by to visit Maudie.'

'So she's living here in the home now, is she?' says Gayle, taking the jacket from me and handing it to Mum. 'Why don't you two find out where she is and take it over?'

'The bell just went for afternoon tea,' says Auntie Iris. 'She might be in the dining room.'

Gayle's grandson runs in from the garden carrying a fistful of flowers he has ripped from their stems. He stands before her, swaying on chubby baby legs, and offers them to her like a prize. 'We'll be escorted off the property, thanks to your vandalism, young man,' she says. He flashes a bright smile and giggles excitedly with all the respect of a two-and-a-half-year-old for adult rules. Gayle takes the flowers with a generous 'Thank you' and throws them back into the flowerbed before the gardener spots them.

I busy myself with a pile of cotton nighties and dressing gowns, all of them covered in messy patterns in the same indistinct floral colours, but my mind is on Gayle. Although I feel close to her in so many ways, she has always been self-contained. I want to know about the changes to her life but we have never shared these confidences before and I don't know how to begin.

'You know Noel and I are separated.' Her directness surprises me. I hastily shake out a nightie and make myself busy refolding it to give me time to gather my thoughts.

'Mum mentioned it. What happened?'

'Nothing much.' From a shelf in the cupboard she lifts down a stack of hand towels trimmed with crocheted edges and still wrapped in cellophane. 'What's the bet these came from one of those charity pick-a-winner stalls?'

'Maudie got all her Christmas gifts there. She gave me a china horse ornament when I was thirteen. It still had the name of the stall on it.'

'You were lucky! When I was ten, I got a set of plastic salad servers.'

Memories of Maudie, they're amongst those small things that bring us together as a family now we are so separated.

'What prompted the break with Noel?' I ask.

'It was coming for a long time. There just wasn't any spark there.'

'Was there ever?' Now it's my directness that surprises me, but I have to admit Noel Keary was a white-bread-sandwich-with-no-seasoning kind of man.

Justin crashes his toy truck into my neat pile of nighties and knocks them into a heap on the floor. 'Uh oh!' he says and quickly turns away.

Gayle retrieves the clothes and begins to refold them. 'I'm sorry he's such a nuisance but I couldn't refuse to take him. This is Simone's regular day off and she misses out on her classes if I cancel. I know what a break meant to me when I had my kids so I can't let her down.' She stacks the pile further up the bed, out of Justin's reach. 'Besides, I love having the little tiger all to myself for a bit.'

She moves between the cupboard and the bed, laying the contents of each shelf out in neat piles so that Mum and Auntie Iris can choose what to keep and what to give away. 'I didn't expect anything when I married Noel. No, that's not true. I expected everything to just fall into place. I thought, You get married, have a family, build a house, do things the way your parents did, and somehow you end up happy.'

'And you didn't?'

'Definitely not! I kept looking for a new activity. I tried crochet and embroidery when I knew I hated doilies. Do you remember those celebration cakes I did? I made a Dolly Varden cake for your . . . What was it?'

'My ninth birthday. It was beautiful. Mum still has the doll.'

'Yeah, and my fondant frangipanis were the best in town. There was money to be made in it but eventually I thought, This isn't filling in time, this is My Life ticking away.'

'What did you want?'

'I wanted It! I just didn't know what It was and I certainly didn't think I had a right to get It. Not then anyway.'

That elusive, mysterious It. My girlfriend Clare talks about It all the time. She spends her life searching for It and sometimes I think she'll die in the process of looking. When I left this town I didn't know what It was either, but I knew I couldn't risk growing old like Maudie. I had to find a life of my own.

'What made the difference?' My question hangs in the air as Gayle searches for the plastic bags to store each of the piles on the bed.

'There's this big haberdashery and craft store out at the Mall. They had a section of folk art materials that I wanted to see.'

Mum talks about the Mall all the time, till it seems like the centre of the universe. Last time I was here it was a plaza, now it's twice the size and it's called the Mall.

'You can spend hours searching for what you want out in that place, it's such a huge barn. Mind you, to some people that can be exciting. I was waiting to be served when this man came buzzing past with a couple of staff in tow. He was talking ten to the dozen and I guarantee he knew every tiny little thing they had in stock, where to find it and how much it cost. I looked at him, and I thought, You live every moment. You really *live* it. It must be wonderful to feel such passion in your life, even for haberdashery. And I knew I just could not go on with Noel. I had to break loose and go in search of what would make me wake up feeling like that.'

GAYLE

The first time I saw Doug Hart was the day I went to Carroll's department store to buy the fabric for my debut frock. I wasn't all that fussed about making my debut but every other girl in my year was saying the same. It was 1960 and the idea of coming out was really a bit old hat. As the time approached, there was suddenly a mad scramble for dressmakers and fabrics and available brothers to partner friends and friends of friends. I swallowed my reticence and joined the other girls for coffee after work at the Chitchat Café to swap plans.

It was Mum who had raised the subject first, after Mass one Sunday.

'The Parish Women's League are organising the Debutante Ball for June 19. There's a notice in the *Catholic Weekly*. We'll have to get cracking if we're going to have your dress ready in time.'

I ran through all the reasons for not making my debut but none of them sounded convincing enough to take into battle with Mum. She had her heart set on my coming out. I prayed for providence to intervene but, as preparations got under way, the chances of a successful intervention slipped further and further into the distance. That's how I found myself waiting for her at Carroll's one lunchtime.

The Special Occasions fabrics were set aside at the back of the store where they were protected from the sweaty fingers of casual passers-by. Carroll's had the best selection in town and everyone came here for their fabrics whether they were choosing for a wedding or for any one of the many balls that dotted the year's social calendar. There was a vast array of materials to suit everyone from the fussiest mother of the bride to the most style-conscious young deb. My parents weren't social. I can't remember them dressing up and going off to a social function. The closest might have been a wedding but usually they stayed in, sitting on either side of the radio listening to whichever show was on at the time. Mostly they chose serials based on detective novels because Dad couldn't stand the comedy shows.

As for myself, I went to Saturday night dances at the Catholic Youth League and met friends at the beer garden along the Strand on Sunday afternoons. If I had to make my debut, I wanted to do it in something modern and elegant and simple.

The most expensive fabrics were imports. They were lined up behind the counter grouped by weight of fabric and in order of colour. They cost the earth and mostly ended up in the lavish wedding gowns of the Italian and Maltese girls from the cane-farming towns to the south. My friend Sandra came from one of those families and I knew that her debut frock would look like something from Princess Margaret's wardrobe.

I studied the less expensive synthetic fabrics. They still

offered an alarming choice. Roll after roll of material leant against the display shelf alongside the blocks of laces and embroidered fabrics. I picked my way through them in search of something suitable. I couldn't picture myself in anything like a wedding dress. I couldn't imagine myself ever getting married, even though that seemed to be everyone's expectation for someone of my age. Auntie Nell was expecting again and wanted me to be godmother. Since I'd turned eighteen, responsibilities had been piling up at my door. Suddenly selecting a debut frock seemed to carry enormous weight, as if a right or wrong choice would have long-standing repercussions.

Noel Keary was to be my escort for the ball. He seemed harmless enough and Mum thought highly of him. She knew his mother and his aunt. In fact she knew his whole family. That was the problem with this damned town. Even strangers in the street knew who I was. I couldn't stop for coffee on the way home from work without Mum knowing every detail before I reached the front door.

I liked strong men: footballers with firm buttocks, though I wouldn't have said that then. Ladies didn't speak like that and it certainly wasn't ladylike to show an interest in a man's rear end. I should have ignored convention and given my instincts more credit. Noel gave the impression of being thin and wiry, although my surreptitious glances noted that his behind was spreading and his tailored work shorts exposed his flabby thighs. It wouldn't have been a major discovery to most people but to me – well, I would have liked to forgive him this discrepancy because he always treated me courteously. In truth, I suspected it revealed an underlying deceitfulness. His upper body pretended to be lean while below the waist he had simply gone to fat. Somehow I thought this suggested a weakness, a dishonesty of character that, try as he might to disguise it, was given away by his physique.

I had put these thoughts out of my mind as the debut ball approached because Noel was the only available partner. He was easily come by since his sister was in my debutantes' group and Mum set up the whole arrangement with his mother. It suited me to put as little effort into this exercise as possible.

And so I found myself in the middle of the display area staring at a roll of ice-white silk satin. It was draped ostentatiously around the body of a store dummy and trailed onto the thick blue pile of the carpet. I always note these details of colour and texture and line. Someone had taken a great deal of care with the folding and flow of the materials. Without thinking, I reached out my hand to stroke the fabric.

'It's got a lovely sheen.'

The voice resonated in my ear with the authority of a guardian angel. I took an instant step backwards and stumbled against a trolley-load of newly arrived fabrics. The pile collapsed. Bolts of fabric spilled across the shop floor, out of the Special Occasions section and onto the linoleum tiles of Affordable Cottons and Prints. I lurched off the trolley in a desperate attempt to grab the last of the rolls as they tumbled, but the force of my movement and the strange twist of my body threw me into the arms of the store dummy. We crashed to the floor in a tangle of satin-swathed limbs. The voice spoke again and I looked up. Through the mess of my hair I could see, standing over me, a solidly built young man, perhaps a year or two older than me. His fair hair was swept back from his face. The top two buttons of his business shirt were undone, allowing a tuft of reddish chest hair to escape. He stretched out a broad hand and, taking mine, lifted me from the jumble of fabric.

'There's no need to fall head over heels,' he said.

I broke into a grin that immediately fell from my face as I looked over his shoulder and saw Mum walking into the store to meet me. He turned his head to follow my glance and broke into his sales pitch without missing a beat. 'We have an excellent range of medium-priced evening fabrics.' I struggled to disguise my nervousness, certain that Mum could read my every gesture. I knew she would be taken aback at the sight of such a flash young man casually chatting to her daughter. I could tell from the way she walked toward us, the tilt of her chin and the habit she had of pulling her jacket together in the front, that she had every intention of getting this over and done with smartly. The young man turned to Mum as she approached and, without addressing her directly, transferred his complete attention to her, leaving me to calm myself in the background.

Mum had a soft spot for young salesmen who were knowledgeable about their products and who treated her with old-fashioned civility. She compared every one she met with Tom Ferguson, the man she considered the master of salesmen and who for years had run the drapery and haberdashery section at Hollis Hopkins with the unmistakable hand of a gentleman.

'Satins are popular this year.' Doug steadied the store dummy. 'They suit the uncluttered lines. There are a couple of lovely georgettes if you're interested in a softer look. And the cream satin has attracted a lot of attention.' As he spoke, Doug cruised between the displays of fabrics, holding up one suggestion after another, pulling bolts of fabric out from under display stands, sweeping his hand across the range of possibilities. Starting with the silks – firm duchesses, smooth satins, light-as-a-feather organzas, chiffons and georgettes – he skimmed quickly over the store's selection of premium fabrics and moved onto the mixes and man-mades. His muscular body propelled itself with ease around the shop fittings. The richly modulated voice introduced each fabric with feeling, caressing it with words. He knew everything about the stuff. How it was made, from what and from where. He even knew how it would cut and make up.

Mum was transfixed by this performance. She could tell that Doug's interest in the merchandise was genuine. He could probably describe the benefits of worsted with as much enthusiasm as he had the delicate materials that attracted our immediate interest. I guessed that he knew every roll of fabric in stock, every card of lace or trim, every colour and grade of sewing cotton, where they had stored the out-of-season pattern books, when the new ranges would arrive. As he served us he called out answers for other staff members who took their queries to him rather than the store manager, who was quietly sipping his tea at the back of the shop. Mum and I were clearly in the best of hands.

We stood in silence. Doug stopped and tucked in a loose end of sheer georgette. He rearranged the flounce of a polyester satin and put the cutting scissors away in a drawer. Still no words came.

'Would you like to look through the pattern books before making a decision?'

Mum sighed with relief as she took a seat on one of the high stools at the pattern table. In front of us was a collection of half a dozen volumes proudly claiming to display the most popular in classic and contemporary styles. I knew exactly what I was looking for but I wanted Mum to be involved in this big decision because, in my mind, the whole event belonged more to her than to me.

'You should have an outfit for the evening too, Mum.' It

would take wild horses to drag Dad to the ball, but if I had to go through with it I was going to make sure he did as well.

'Don't be silly. I'll just be a bystander.'

'I don't mean a ball gown, but something to feel like you're dressing up.'

She reached out and took one of the books, resolutely opening it at evening wear. 'We'd better get down to it, my girl,' she said. 'Your lunch break's running out.'

It took twenty-five minutes to decide on a full-skirted dress that would show off my small waist. It had cap sleeves and a scalloped neckline – high enough for Mum's sense of modesty. We chose a bone-white polyester satin for the fabric and I convinced Mum to buy a length of white fur fabric that would make two stoles, one for me and one to dress up her cream bouclé suit.

Doug slipped his scissors through the fabric. In deft swoops he folded it into a neat, paper-wrapped parcel that he carried to the sales counter in the centre of the store.

Mum looked at her watch. 'You'll be late,' she said. 'Go on. I'll take care of this.'

I dropped a kiss on her cheek. 'Thanks for the dress, Mum.'

She dabbed at the corner of her eye and dived into her handbag for her purse. Doug entered the purchase details onto the docket and rang up the sale. As I walked down the main aisle to the front door of the store, I felt like my stiletto heels were tapping out a reply.

IRIS

'I saw Mavis McCarthy the other day.'

Nell wriggles around in her chair as I speak. Her feet are hurting. I can tell by the way she puts them together and pushes forward on her toes. Any moment now she will slip her shoes off and rub the toes of one foot over and around the bunion that's causing the most pain. We've both got bad feet. We got them from Mum. She blamed hers on so much standing around on cold, hard floors when she was a barmaid. Mine? I reckon it was those fashion shoes we wore when we were young. We both wore them, Nell and I.

The kitchen staff reach our side of the sitting room with a tea trolley and freshly baked scones and Anzac biscuits. They don't do them as well as my Anzac biscuits but at my time of life I'd rather be waited on than fuss about that. Generally the staff are nice but sometimes they get a bit short. It must be difficult spending all day, every day looking after a bunch of old folk, with some of them doing nothing but squabble.

Lately Nell hasn't been herself. She's preoccupied and sometimes absent-minded, which is not like her. She's usually right on top of things but she's got a sentimental streak, our Nell, and she's always fussed over Maudie. All this coming and going must be wearing her down.

It bothers me that Nell is over there all by herself in that place on the Island, but she won't hear of moving into the nursing home. She can be stubborn about some things. I'm very comfortable, and the staff here have taken good care of Maudie over the last few years.

There wouldn't be a problem if Kate lived up here but that's not likely to happen. Nell's only got herself to blame. She didn't give young Kate room to breathe. They did everything together. The girl had to get away if she was to have a life of her own. I tried to tell Nell that she couldn't cloister Kate but she couldn't see it. You can't live your life through your children, or spend your time running around expecting the worst and trying to prevent it. You have to let them grow or you'll lose them forever.

Nell slips her shoe back on and looks up at me.

'You know, Mavis McCarthy,' I prompt. 'Her sister married Jimmy Adcock and they lived down there in Railway Estate. Off Railway Terrace.'

'You mean that old low-set place that used to get flooded every year?'

Nell can be a dark one at times but she doesn't easily fool me and she doesn't easily forget an injury. I could tell she remembered Mavis but she had her reasons for being cagey.

NELL

Railway Terrace. Jack and I rented a place there when the boys were little. We started off in a flat down the road from Mum's. During the war, when I was expecting our first son, Gerald, and Jack was away fighting, I moved in to live with his parents. They had a big home with plenty of room for us to stay if we had wanted to, but once the war was over and our family was growing we needed to be out on our own. Jack wanted to be master of his own home, not answering to his dad all the time. I was pleased to be in our own place. Jack's mother was the perfect housekeeper and she liked to see her beautiful things out on display. You can't do that with little ones about. When young Gerry started to crawl, I had to follow him around her house ready to catch anything he might topple over. I couldn't rest a minute living under her roof with the boys.

'I saw her yesterday.'

'Who?'

'Mavis McCarthy. Haven't you been listening to a word I've been saying?'

I remember Mavis McCarthy all right. When I was working in the office at the hospital, Mavis had a position with McKimmin's, the drapers. She was in our social group at the church. I think she had her eye on Jack for a while, just around the time he was starting to take an interest in me.

One of our regular excursions was up to the Bohle River. We would hire open trucks for the day and leave town early in the morning to get up there before the sun got too strong. The Bohle was a good place for a picnic day. The river was fresh running but only in parts of the riverbed. Most of it was sandy islands. Each group set up a camp and made a billy of tea and pulled out the picnic food. We spent the day swimming, walking through the nearby bush and wandering between the camps, catching up with friends. At least thirty or forty people went each time.

Mavis McCarthy was a regular at the picnics. She came with a group of people that Iris knew. That's how Iris came to overhear what Mavis had to say about me. She made a comment that suggested I was having indecent relations with one of the young doctors at the hospital. It was disgusting and nothing could have been further from the truth! The office was well away from the wards, in a separate cottage. We never even saw the doctors! It was hurtful. We were modest young women. We didn't compromise ourselves. When you didn't have a father to look out for you, you had to be even more careful than the next girl, and Mum was always strict about our behaviour. When Iris heard about this, she took up the matter and challenged Mavis over it till she backed down and apologised.

It was Iris who twigged to the fact that Mavis was sweet on Jack and jealous of his interest in me.

IRIS

After Dad died and we moved to the south side, Mum enrolled us at the convent. That's where Mavis first came into the picture. She had plaits she could sit on and her legs were so long, we called her beanpole. She was the best runner in the school and it seemed like everything Mavis McCarthy did was perfect. Except she was a sneak.

There was the time she tried to come between Nell and Jack by soiling Nell's reputation, but it was worse when Phyll got in the family way.

Mavis had a sister, Dot, who started nursing at the hospital with Phyll. They were so short of staff during the war that once a nurse started training she wasn't allowed to leave unless she was pregnant or joined the army. Well, when Phyll left, Dot knew she wasn't joining the army. It didn't take too much for her to put two and two together but that didn't give Mavis any right to go about spreading stories. Phyll wasn't a tart like Mavis tried to make out. She had an unfortunate experience, that's all, and she paid for it all right. But Mavis gave the impression that she found out from me. It took a long time for Phyll and I to sort that one out, and by then the damage was too far gone.

In all these years I've hardly set eyes on Mavis. At first I didn't recognise her at the Mall the other day. I was sitting near the fountain waiting for Gayle to drive me home. The old lady opposite looked familiar but it took me a while to realise it was Mavis. She's aged, all right. She was such a tall young woman. Now she's all bent over, and having trouble with her feet, too, I'd say. There was a walking-frame beside her and she was by herself. I heard once that she married Ernie McAllister's cousin, Fred, but it ended badly, so she's had her share of shame, too.

I felt sad seeing her sitting there, poor old thing. Fancy coming to that – old, crippled and alone. We all started out with grand plans and big ideas and no idea where time would take us. At least Maudie and Phyll and Nell and I have kept together in one fashion or another. I thought about going up to Mavis and speaking, but what would I say? I never liked her. It would be hypocritical to pretend we could share old memories.

No, better to leave well enough as it is.

KATE

The rain sets in the day after I arrive. There is little that can be done at the hospital. Maudie is comfortable, her condition unchanged. Mum had come over with only enough clothes for a short stay so we decide to go home for the time being.

Uncle Vic drives us down to the ferry terminal and carries my bags to the loading port. He says he doesn't like hanging about in town and will it be all right if he leaves us there, under the awning, to wait for the boat.

By the time we arrive home, the weather still has not let up. Slow, steady, reassuring rain. A curtain encircling the house, enclosing us in a small world, together. We move about to the steady drumming on the corrugated-iron roof and the light scratch of water hitting the gravel in the yard. They are round, comforting sounds. I like it when it rains here. It brings a pleasant coolness and reminds me of childhood holidays in the rainforests up north.

We have lunch and Mum lies down for her afternoon nap.

I sit on the floor in front of the old bookcase and pull out ancient books, some from my childhood and others accumulated from my older brothers and parents and uncles and aunts. I begin a drawing and take up the whole of the table with my sketches and crayons. I start things and move on, leaving a trail of works-in-progress behind me. Whenever I come to the Island, I bring things to keep me occupied. It is as if I must bring some of my immediate surroundings with me, as if I cannot bear to leave home without my grown-up toys, my books, sewing, drawing paper, crayons and notebooks. These are not projects to be finished. They are to be worked on endlessly, never completed – friends to keep me company, to fill the hours that I spend here inside this house. It's my quiet obsession and the family photos are swept aside to make way for the things I unload from my suitcase.

The hours pass by, with us cocooned by the rain. Mum does shepherd's pie for dinner and watches *Catchphrase* while the mashed-potato topping browns in the oven. She loves crosswords and word games, and from my possie in the dining room I hear her shouting out her contributions, as if they might help the contestant she's chosen to back tonight.

By nine o'clock Mum sits slumped like a little dumpling doll in her recliner rocker. Her eyes keep closing over as she tries to follow the television. This is her nightly ritual of trying to stay awake just a little bit longer, so that when she finally goes to bed she sleeps right through the night. I get up to make a cup of tea and she stirs.

'Is the door deadlocked?' she says.

'It's okay.'

'No, it isn't!' Her voice takes on that insisting tone. We've been through this before and she just won't let it slide. 'Will you lock it, please.'

'It's all right. It's only nine o'clock.'

'Well, that's late enough.' Her chin drops to her neck. She stretches her legs and studies her toes as she tries to get me to do her bidding. 'I don't want anybody breaking in. I want to sleep soundly tonight.'

'Don't be silly. No one's going to be out in this rain.'

'Rain or no rain, if they're going to try it I'd rather the door's locked. I want to feel safe.'

'You can't get in from the outside without a key anyway.'

'I don't care. You never know who's around the streets these days. You see these things on the news. Some poor old lady attacked in her home. People think they're all right until something happens to them.'

'You always think the worst. The door doesn't have to be deadlocked when we're here. What if there's a fire?'

She has to put both feet on the floor and grasp each side of the armchair to pull herself up and out of the seat. It takes her a moment to steady herself.

'Fire or not, I just don't want to be murdered in my bed. When you get to my age, you know things happen. You can't be too careful.'

'Don't be silly. Go and sit down. You're not going to lock us up in some prison.'

She sits back down but I know she's not happy. From the kitchen I can feel her moving forward on her chair, chin on her hand, looking intently at a spot halfway between herself and the television screen. I wash the dinner dishes noisily and make more of that stream of tea we consume constantly, cup by delicate china cup. She knows me so well. She hears how busy I am and knows that the busier I am, the more that door lock sits on my mind. The crazy thing is, it's not really about whether the door is locked.

She just wants to feel safe, and if having the door locked makes her happy, why can't I just do it?

I scrape a plate so hard I nearly take the pattern as well. I know very well why I am so stubborn about the lock. *You're always doing this to me. Making me feel afraid, afraid to sleep without a locked door. Pushing me to lock bits and pieces of my life away in case they get stolen, afraid to do this, not to do that. Don't trust . . . Lock up . . . Secure away . . . Wear your life on a bunch of keys around your waist. Live behind bars, with yourself as the jailer. Rules. Fears. You taught me to be afraid, to be a timid little scaredy-cat. Every day the fear rises and falls like a tide and, like the tide, it never goes away. I'm scared to walk out of my own front door. It takes me three or four goes to get to the bus stop. I worry I've left the iron on or not locked the windows. I'm frightened I've forgotten something or that I won't get through the day without something bad happening. Even the reassuring bulge of money in my purse can't quell the panic. And every time I buck your caution – I take some small, simple risk like crossing the road against the lights – somehow your incessant warnings trim my sails and I hurry in case a car comes round the corner.*

At eleven o'clock she's lying in bed but she's not asleep. I know she's not asleep. She's lying there counting the beads on the rosary, whispering the words of the Hail Marys, the Our Fathers. I tiptoe to the back door. I clasp the second key dangling from the key chain so the two won't bump against each other and give me away with their jangling. Soundlessly I move my weight on the floorboards and turn the key in the deadlock. *Clack*. The latch turns over loudly. Damn! She'll have heard. She's been lying there waiting for some sound from inside or out. I hear her stir. There's the sound of the metal cross on her rosary clinking onto the glass top of the bedside table and her body settling back onto the mattress, and soon her soft, breathy snores come regularly, one after another.

I wake early. The mango tree in the backyard shadows this corner of the house from the morning sun. In summer it's a blessing, protecting the rooms from the first blaze of heat. Today it sets a chill in the room, making it pleasant to lie here under the light covers. The garden is filled with the noise of birds feeding in the morning cool. I lie still, eyes closed. Thoughts drift in and out.

Daniel.

In Sydney Dan sleeps beside me. He stirs. His hand brushes mine. I turn my head to rest on his shoulder. His skin smells of . . . of him. I once read that each person is marked by an individual scent, like an identifying smell. Dan's scent is open, ozone-like, a smell of sleep, not of sweat. It's comforting. I nuzzle into him but smell only the traces of Mum's linen-cupboard camphor on the pillow. Dan's in Sydney and I'm here. Outside the louvres the birds squawk and squeal in the bush, shaking and scraping its branches against the glass as they fight over the bright, nectar-filled hibiscus.

It was my idea to try in-vitro. Dan was happy to fall in with my decision. He came to the clinic. He answered the questions. He signed the forms. He ejaculated on demand. He didn't complain. Once we had agreed to go ahead, we didn't talk about it. But inside I knew that for him it would be so much easier with someone who could fall pregnant on call.

We've had three goes. Three times hoping, three times doing everything right, three times being let down. Warnings don't prepare you for the crumpling disappointment. They tell you not to hope too much, but what is hope? I have come to see its slender thread in waiting, in possibility, and in trying again and again. The letdown is hard.

I called the halt. I needed time to think, to mull over the endless stream of questions that crawled sideways through my head, leaving me more confused each time I tried to resolve them.

The birds settle their differences and as they bounce from flower to flower drinking in the sweetness the branches scratch the glass lightly. I try to imagine Dan as a dad. I picture him changing a nappy, coaching his son or daughter from the sidelines, rolling around in the grass, laughing. They're like scenes from a movie in which Dan plays the good dad. I know this man. He is considerate. He always does what is expected of him. He never lets people down, but none of this tells me what I need to know.

I hear Mum's slippered footfall on the polished wooden

floorboards as she moves slowly, with the stiffness of morning. Water runs in the kitchen sink, the kettle gives a low rumble as it goes on the boil, teacups and cereal bowls chink as they are set on the table. If I'm lucky she'll squeeze bush oranges for juice.

Coming home was a relief, an excuse to take a break, space to think.

We just went for it, Dan and I. At the clinic we gave the right answers to all the questions. Yes, we really want a family. Yes, we have the means to care for this child. No one asked if I would make a good mother, if I thought I could do it well. No one asked if Dan was doing this just to please me.

The juice is the thin colour of lemon water but it has the strongest, sweetest orange flavour. I run it around my teeth so as not to swallow it too quickly. There's freshly cooked porridge with a thin crust of sugar, and toast with rosella jam. Its taste is tart and familiar.

'Where did you get the jam?'

'The school had a stall on the esplanade. I looked for lemon butter, then I saw that instead.'

The jam brings back memories of late afternoons spent picking the strange, red flower-fruits that grow wild on the spare allotment at the back of the bay, and the sticky mass bubbling away in battered old camping saucepans, the white froth skimmed from the top of the pot, and the front of my dress stained with the telltale dark red juice.

This was something that Mum and I did on holidays when Dad and the boys were off at work, engaged in sales and commerce and management and the sort of men's business that I am now a part of with my job. Looking back at our domestic activity, it seems so frivolous, a mother teaching her daughter her secret for perfect jam.

' How did you feel about being a mum?'

'What do you mean?'

'Like, when you had Gerry, how did it feel? Were you really excited?'

'I don't know about excited. I was pleased.'

'Yeah, but he was your first child. Was it special?'

'You were all special, in your own way.'

'I don't mean, Were we special? I mean, Was it a special experience for you . . . to be a mother?'

'I suppose so, but I didn't question my motives for everything the way you do.'

I stop for a moment. It had never occurred to me that I gave these things more consideration than other people did. There are things we do unconsciously and things we do in a detached and studied way. My way is to study all the whys and wherefores before I follow through and when I have to make a choice, I consistently weigh up all the benefits and obstacles and repercussions. No wonder I drive myself insane with indecision.

'You were my big surprise,' says Mum in a singsong voice.

'But at the beginning did you plan to have children?'

Mum chews her toast very slowly. She hates anything that comes anywhere near a suggestion of sex and she had not foreseen that the conversation would go this far. She fingers the handle of her worn china teacup cautiously and sips a mouthful of tea to help her swallow.

'We wanted a family.'

'Yes, but did you plan when and how many? Or did you just let it happen?'

'You shouldn't be asking. It's private.' For a moment I think she will refuse to go on. Then the cup clatters in its saucer and her mouth twists in an attempt to be lighthearted. 'We didn't question it. You were all gifts from God. I couldn't send you back.' She presses her fingers onto the crumbs that have fallen around her plate and lifts them back.

'But did you think about what it meant to have children? Did you question whether you could be a good mother?' I push on despite the growing tightness in her voice.

'You were all looked after well. You had good schooling and a nice home. You always had new clothes.'

'I'm not asking about warm baths and hot dinners. I mean how you'd guide us, what values you'd teach us.'

'You were given good values.' She finds more crumbs that I can't see and scrapes them into her hand. 'Though sometimes what you've done with them I'd like to know.' Her words find their mark but I don't react. There is no point diverting into an argument about why Dan and I live together. Before she continues she wipes her hands, dusting the crumbs onto the plate. 'We practised our values then, not like today. People say they can't cope and they expect to be let off the hook. We had responsibilities and we stuck with them. We didn't just give up.'

On the sideboard behind her my mother's face glows through the sepia tones of her wedding photo and matches the soft satin sheen of her gown. Dad stands straight and proud beside her, his collar and cuffs starched to perfection against his morning suit.

I search for ways to explain what it is that I need to know. I have to ask her because who else can help me understand this confusion? 'What about making the right decisions, teaching us good judgement?'

'We taught you right from wrong. And we had our religion.' She picks up her teacup and looks at the underside, as if reading the maker's mark for the first time. Again she tries to be light-hearted. 'You've neglected that. When was the last time you went to confession?'

I can't remember and I know I don't care. Giving up Mass was my first act of defiance, so long ago now that to reverse it would feel like changing my citizenship.

The rain has cleared overnight and the sun is quickly warming up the day. It seems like a good opportunity to escape and on the spur of the moment I forge a plan to walk one of the bush tracks.

'In that case, I'll go to seniors,' she says. A flash of guilt surges through me. I realise she was planning to miss her weekly seniors club meeting to be with me, and without thinking I have excluded her. I kick myself for being thoughtless but I need the space to think.

I miss the views from the bush track as I stride along, oblivious to everything but the old stories that fill my mind, the past conflicts, the feeling of not being allowed to think my own thoughts, make my own choices, have my own life. If I had a daughter, would I use her the same way? Shape and mould her to fill Dan's space when he's gone? Would I give her life only to try to prune that life into the shape that suited me? I want time to unravel all these confused thoughts and fears about having a child with Dan, and instead my mind is full of guilt for giving myself space instead of spending time with my mother. I'm angry with her and angry with myself. Twigs snap under the stamp of my feet. The air rings with a curlew's pitiful cry. The bush is empty of people. Everything conspires to remind me that she's old and fragile and alone.

I manage everything else in my life. I take responsibility for my job, for my part in our home, our partnership. Why is it that anything I do with Mum comes tagged with guilt? Mum cannot give me the reassurance that I would not repeat what Nana did with Maudie, and she can't recognise that she herself tried to do the same with me. I just know I couldn't bear to raise a child, a daughter, who spends her life running from me.

I think that with Dan I could take the risk, but I can't sense his presence any more. He's a dream, part of the life I wish I had. To my despair, I have sunk so quickly back into the life I have always tried to escape from that he has slipped away. Today my reality is the bush, the Island, Mum – and the smell of camphor.

There was a bush orange tree in Nana's backyard. Although it had a good shape, it was stunted and looked more like a lemon tree than an orange. It had grey-green leaves that were always covered with a dirty film, like a fungus or scale. It didn't stop the tree from bearing the most delicious fruit I have ever eaten. When the crop was on, the tree was covered in fruit with the shape of oranges but the pale green-yellow colour of lemons. The first time Nana cut one for me, I squinced up my face at the thought of the tartness that would fur my teeth.

'Try it,' she said.

I hesitated.

'Go on.'

I looked at her. She studied the knife she was wiping.

'You'll like it. It's sweet.'

Nana wasn't one to cajole or encourage. She just said, and that was that. I knew she'd cut this orange just for me. Its neat quarters lay on the plate with their fleshy tips pointing invitingly upwards. There was no one else in the house. Maudie was at work. Mum was shopping in town.

Auntie Phyll had taken her boys to the pool. I was the only one little enough to need minding, which is how I came to be sitting on the high stool in Nana's kitchen, hesitating over an orange. It was one of those small treats like the eggflips Mum and I shared on special afternoons.

Nana bent over a drawer, searching for something amongst the cooking knives and egg-rings. I dipped my finger into the puddle of juice that had spilt on the plate and lifted a drop onto my tongue. The sweetness hit me instantly.

'They're deceptive, those oranges,' she said. 'They don't waste time on outside appearances. Everything goes into the juice.'

She stood back from the drawer, holding a strange-looking implement. It had a metal handle and a coiled metal head that sprang back when she released it from the palm of her hand. 'It's a sort of beater,' she said. 'I'm going to make custard for tea.' I often investigated the kitchen drawer, fascinated by Nana's collection of cooking tools. She had ageing forks with tines sharp enough to stab a raw potato, and bone-handled butter knives that had been worked against the sharpening steel over so many years that they were worn down to sharp little stubs. I tried to use the hand- beaters but couldn't grasp the trick needed to stop them from jamming. We had nothing like these in Mum's kitchen, where the electric frypan and Sunbeam MixMaster stood on the kitchen bench under custom-made covers waiting for their next use, and where the cupboards were full of plastic storage containers.

I picked up an orange quarter with my stubby fingers and sucked hard. Juice exploded into my mouth and I couldn't swallow quickly enough. It stung the top of my airway and spilled out of my mouth and nostrils and filled my eyes with tears. A tiny wee escaped. As I squeezed in my muscles to catch it, I coughed and lost my balance on the stool. I flung out my hand to grab the table but at that moment I coughed again, so hard that – it was too late. The gush saturated my panties and ran down my legs to the floor.

'There's no need to get excited about it,' said Nana. She slapped me between the shoulderblades and wiped my eyes with the corner of her kitchen towel.

'I wet myself, Nana.' The words came out, half sobs, half choking gulps for air.

'Well, you'd have to be a blind priest not to see that,' she said.

The lean-to laundry outside the kitchen had big concrete laundry tubs where I squatted while Nana sponged me down. The front door slammed hard.

'That'll be Maudie,' she said as she lifted me out. 'We might just say you had a bit of a buster and wanted a bath. No need for details.'

Maudie spilled the contents of her bag over the kitchen table and threw herself into a chair. She grinned as I entered, and leaned forward to prod my towel-clad stomach. 'Gidday, ragamuffin,' she said. 'You smell like a cashmere bouquet.'

Nana interrupted her immediately, waving her arm in the direction of the table. 'Now look at that mess,' she said. 'You've been home two minutes and already I can't set a teacup on that table.'

'All right. All right. All right.' With each word Maudie's voice went up a note. She swung her arms and swept her possessions back into the bag. 'It's not the worst crime in the world.'

'Just settle down, Maudie.' The tone of Nana's voice was even, not betraying a single emotion. 'There's no need to get into a tizz.'

'There wouldn't be if you stopped picking on me.' Maudie clasped her oversized bag to her chest and flounced out of the room. The walls shook with the stamp of her feet as she stormed through the house and into the bedroom.

A sudden quiet descended on the house.

'Can I come in?' My mother stood at the back door. Her voice punctuated the stillness.

Nana turned to me. 'Why don't you tell Maudie I've put the kettle on if she wants a cup of tea?'

Nana's house was an old miner's cottage that had been transported to the south side when it was a flourishing suburb. Two huge Bowen mango trees sheltered the front verandah and kept the interior cool even on the hottest of summer days. Maudie's room was at the front of the house, off the living room. A three-quarter length of curtaining screened the doorway and drifted in and out in the breeze. Maudie was sprawled across the bed, sorting out the contents of her bag.

'Whatderyerwant, Mrs Muggins?'

'Mum's here and Nana's making tea if you want some.'

I wandered over to her dresser. It was laden with boxes and bowls of cheap costume jewellery.

'Do you want to try on my beads?'

I fingered a string of white plastic beads interspersed with little red and blue beads. The matching earrings were clusters of white, red and blue. I handed them to her.

'They're clip-ons. They'll hurt your ears,' she warned.

'I don't care.'

'I bought some new beads today.'

She tore open the crisp new paper bag from Coles and let the bright crimson baubles spill across the bedcover. Maudie's laugh gurgled up from deep inside her and burst out in a cackle that was heedless of her surroundings. As I grew older, I discovered the acute embarrassment her eccentricities could cause in public, but for the moment she was an equal, the only adult in my life who could be approached without reservation or awe.

We caused a sensation when we turned up for tea. Nana called us a 'flash pair' and Mum took a photo of us with our crimson beads and rouged cheeks and our scarlet lips and handbags over our arms.

NELL

The back shed is where I store a lot of my old things. There's not enough room in the house and I like things to be uncluttered these days. Sometimes I get a bit wonky on my feet and I like to have lots of space around me. After Kate left for her walk, I thought of that old chest I stored up in the shed. She always liked that and I've been meaning to get it down for her. It wasn't heavy, just a bit awkward to juggle when you're on a stepladder.

People keep telling me I shouldn't do so much and I have let a lot of things go but I like to be active and independent. I may be getting on but I'm not totally useless.

The turns come infrequently. I can never predict them. They come on like a dizzy spell. I feel as if I might fall if I don't sit down, and when I come to I'm very disoriented. It takes a few minutes to work out where I am, and they leave me feeling breathless. My doctor says it's my heart, a slow leak like a time bomb. Nothing we can do except take an aspirin each day to keep the blood from thickening.

I forgot it today when I went to the shed. I didn't expect to be that long and I was thinking about the chest.

If Kate had been around I would have got her to lift the blessed thing down but she went off on that walk. I was disappointed. I cancelled my seniors morning to spend it with her and she goes off traipsing all around the Island by herself. She can be a selfish girl sometimes. She has something on her mind, I can tell that, but Kate always has something on her mind. She's always been preoccupied with things that other people just let lie. 'Why do you have to waste time worrying over things like that?' I ask her. 'Just get on with your life and leave things to work themselves out.' But no, she has to dig away at it with a spoon.

She got a fright when she saw me sitting on the chair and struggling to catch my breath. I could hear it in her voice, all squeaky and childlike. 'Mum,' she said. 'What is it? What's wrong?' I hadn't told anyone before, certainly not Vic or Phyll. They're on at me already to leave here and move into a home. I just want to be left in peace for whatever time I have left. If I have to go, I'd rather do it here in my own home, in my own time, like Jack did, peacefully in his sleep.

Kate feels that she should come home to look after me. I'd like that but I know she can't. She has a job and a life in Sydney. Then there's Dan, but she puts too much into that for my liking. It isn't as if they're married, and in my books they shouldn't be living together. It's sinful but you can't tell Kate. She's obstinate. At least she hasn't presented me with a grandchild out of wedlock. I don't want any of those.

KATE

I came back and found her sitting there in that chair, pale and confused, not like Mum at all. It was all my worst nightmares happening at once, those small dark fears that you push to the back corners of your mind. There was something about the way she brushed off my questions about her health. I don't know what it was, I just sensed that something was wrong.

She was unsteady on her feet as I guided her to the toilet and I had to stay close by so I could help her to the bathroom and into bed. She keeps saying she's all right and only has a headache. She took an aspirin and I put a damp face washer across her forehead to cool her.

I leave her to sleep and soon enough the low whistle, which comes at the tail end of each snore, tells me she is dozing. I creep back into the room and watch her to reassure myself that she is all right.

The glory box that Dad gave her for an engagement

present sits along one wall of her bedroom. A discreetly elaborate wooden inlay graces the lid, still so highly polished I can see my reflection, and it is hinged so it opens like a trunk. The box used to stand on long legs that were curved in the most exaggerated way. I had to pull the dressing-table stool across and climb up on it to be high enough to peer inside. In the seventies, when Mum modernised their lives, she had Dad drop the height by replacing those elegant legs with stout ones from the building section of K-mart.

I loved my mother's glory box. It was where she kept all her private and precious things and I thought of it as one of our shared secrets, like the thickly rich eggnogs drunk from fat cut-crystal glasses. Mum's, I suspect, was laced with something stronger than the vanilla essence that she put in mine.

We had a ritual to follow when Mum decided to open the box. Hands had to be washed, dirty play clothes changed, and the bedspread folded back from the bottom of the bed so things could be laid out carefully on the white cotton sheet. At first I was happy enough to explore what immediately caught my eye – collections of cards, school reports and eisteddfod certificates, odd knitting needles, broken necklaces, and the slender china girl, a twenties flapper, draped across the velvet mound of a pincushion.

One time I discovered there was deeper treasure. My mother was searching for something she had stored well out of reach. She bent over into the box, took hold of two handles and lifted out a tray. The long-trapped vapours of camphor balls burst into my face, and from the hidden section below she carefully lifted layer after layer and spread them out on the bed. The hand-stitched matinee jackets and baby layettes decorated with the almost imperceptible stitches of Richelieu work, which she had made when expecting Gerry, were wrapped in tissue paper, their shiny cream silk now browning with age and spotted with tiny holes where the fabric had worn. There was an evening dress and a fine shawl, and old concert programs, my first communion veil, a length of my hair saved from the hairdresser's floor, and the head of my first doll with its exotic Spanish looks. That doll was a beautiful, finely proportioned creature and I loved her deeply, even as I pulled her insides apart to see what made her cry 'Mama'.

They are all still there. I go through the box and pull them out one by one, laying them carefully on the bed beside where she sleeps. The smell of camphor swells in the humid air.

'What are you doing there?' My mother speaks in the slurry tones of sleep.

'It's okay,' I say. 'I'll put it all back.'

'Just so long as you do.' She rolls over and immediately falls asleep again.

I fold and tuck and lay things back in the box. I don't want to explore further. The spell is broken but I find I can't be irritated with her. When I wanted to run and gather clouds in my arms my mother said, 'Don't fall.' When I wanted to throw myself into the big round waves that rushed right up to the beach line, my mother said, 'Stay in the enclosure.' My childhood was littered with her don'ts. In my adolescence they became life rules, set in concrete. Don't wear halter-neck dresses, you'll get a chill in the kidneys. Don't walk around barefoot, you'll get piles. Don't use tampons, you'll get pneumonia. Don't wear high-heels when you're pregnant or the baby will be born crippled. Poor crippled babies, poor speechless doll, poor sick Mum lying there worn out and crumpled on the bed.

The best view of our bay is from the lookout on the hill on the northern side, from a place where two huge granite rocks balanced one on top of the other give the impression of a giant thumb sticking up in the air. I have no idea how it got its name but all my life it has been known as Tom Thumb. As a child I was allowed the run of our bay. I could go anywhere I wanted within the arms of the headlands, except for Tom Thumb. Mum was worried that one day the rocks would overbalance and crush anyone who happened to be standing in the way.

I was an obedient child. I did most things I was instructed to do and avoided most things I was told to avoid without finding the restrictions overly constraining, but Tom Thumb sat so enticingly up on the hill and despite my repeated requests to be taken up there, Mum resisted. She didn't like the steep walk and she was not fond of heights and, most of all, she was frightened that the rock might fall. I didn't deliberately want to disobey my mother. I knew she was concerned for my wellbeing but every time we came to the Island, Tom Thumb was sitting there on the hill looking down at me, tempting me. Our visitors would go up there and come back with faces glowing from the brisk walk and the fresh breeze at the top but I was not allowed to join them. I had to satisfy myself with creating pictures of the view from their descriptions and the occasional photo that one of them mailed back to Mum.

One day the latest visitors were cooling down from their walk, sitting on the back verandah that Dad had built onto the hut. Mum brought out icy lemon cordial and beer and they talked over the top of each other, describing what it was like from up there. As usual I was hanging round the back of Mum's chair and following her in and out of the kitchen, until she nearly tripped over.

'For goodness sakes, Katey, get out from under my feet! Find something to occupy yourself with for five minutes.'

'Can I go for a walk?'

'So long as you stay in the bay. You know the rules.'

I grabbed an orange from the kitchen and my thongs from under the bed and was out the door before Mum could change her mind.

The walk up to Tom Thumb started at the back of the bay, near the road that led over the hill to the rest of the Island. The track was well marked, though rough and steep. After a few steps I was perspiring heavily and I couldn't see the object of my acute interest. I pulled out my orange, bit into the skin at the top and forced my thumb-nail underneath so I could pull the skin off in chunks. The juice ran out as I pulled the orange apart and I held it away from my body to let the drops fall in the thick black dust.

My heart started to thump inside my chest wall and already my determination to reach the rock was flagging. Norfolk Island pines were scattered thinly along the ridge of the hill, and the feet of many sightseers had ground the needles into the thick carpet coating the track. Through the sparse vegetation I could see into the backyards of the huts that ran up to the base of the hill and I hoped desperately that I would not be spotted by someone who knew my mother well enough to mention later that they'd seen me. A kookaburra landed on a branch and I leapt in fright as his raucous laugh rang out from the tree right above me. It seemed as though he were telling on me as loudly as he could, screaming the news of my disobedience across the bay.

A thin vibration of fear ran through me. What if he was warning me? What if Mum was right? The rock was unstable and the moment I set foot on the flat land around it my step would set off a current of movement that would topple it over, sending it crushing down on me. I wouldn't be able to get out of it then. Mum would find out and I would be in very big strife.

With this scenario playing in my mind, I was oblivious to the rest of the walk until I rounded a tree and stepped into the clearing where Tom Thumb sat in front of me. The buzzing of cicadas filled my head so I couldn't think properly, or maybe it was just that I was dizzy with fear. The rock itself was not so high but it still stood well above me. I reached out a sticky hand and laid it against the stone face, and immediately pulled it away again. My body was vibrating with the sound, or with shock at my audacity. I stood in a place where I was half concealed by the rock but could still look down on the flat middle of the bay where our house stood. Our visitors had talked of the view being so high up that the people below looked like ants. It wasn't true! It was now the middle of the day and only a few people were walking about in the open but I could see them clearly. To my surprise I could make out the three distinct figures sitting on our back verandah, and I watched as Mum stood and walked into the house and came back carrying something that I guessed was the platter of sandwiches she had made earlier. I suddenly realised that it must be time for lunch and I was hungry.

My legs trembled so much that I had to hold onto the trees as I started the downward climb, and more than once my thongs slid so that I nearly fell. Halfway down

I detoured from the track to squat behind a fallen tree overgrown with sticky vine. My wee squirted onto the ground and splashed my dusty feet, leaving spots of wetness that more dust clung to once I started walking again. I could still feel a knot of fear as I walked round the paw-paw trees to where the visitors were sitting in the shade at the back of the house.

'What have you been up to?' Mum asked.

'Nothing,' I said, grabbing the last pink salmon sandwich from the platter.

PHYLL

Fear. Fear of losing. Loss of feeling.

When they took her out of my arms and gave her to Iris, I lost all feeling. It took days for any sensation to come into my body. I was numb from head to toe and when the feeling did return, it was like pins and needles, this prickling, all over. It nearly drove me crazy. It was like the nerve ends were scratching against each other under my skin.

I have been a scratcher ever since. If I get an itch, I can't stop myself. It drives Vic mad when he sees me do it.

'You'll tear yourself to pieces,' he says, but I can't stop.

Iris held out her arms to take my baby but her eyes didn't move. They couldn't. She had just come from tending her own baby, a living, breathing bundle that moved when she touched it and cried with hunger. How could she wrap her arms around my poor still baby and look into my face without giving away the relief she must have felt that it was mine that had died and hers that lived? And what relief! I could hear them saying, 'It was all for the best, poor fatherless mite.'

Iris was good with the baby, I'll give her that. She handled it well, as she should have, with two children of her own already, not counting the little newborn sleeping next door. She even wrapped the child in a blanket she had knitted for her own. A pink blanket for a little girl, but it was a job well done, not a labour of love. I cried for my mother then. I should have been near her, and if it hadn't been for Iris and Nell and their respectable notions I would have been. They thought by the time I had carried the baby full term I would want to keep it. At first it wasn't a baby to me, just a thing that that man had planted inside me, the way he'd forced himself. The very thought of it made me retch; I just wanted to tear this thing out.

We went to Auntie Lizzie's farm for the confinement, up in the mountain range behind Tully, far enough away to keep our doings secret. Iris insisted on it. She dreamt up a story that she was ill. 'We can say that I need to rest and Phyll is with me for the company,' she told Mum and Nell.

'No hint of scandal, no questions asked. People will think it's natural. After all, she's been doing her nursing training.' Iris was carrying her third. I was a few weeks behind her. We left home before I started to show.

Auntie Lizzie was an angel. She made me feel well looked after. No fuss, no bother, no judgements, but a lot of caring. They were right. As the baby started to grow, things did change. I started to think of it as a baby. I felt it moving and once or twice I even caught myself talking to it. Auntie Lizzie knitted a layette and when I opened the drawer and looked at those garments, those tiny cream bootees and the delicate woollen bonnet, I felt something stir in my heart.

It was a difficult birth. The pain was sharp and the muscle spasms seared through me. She struggled. I struggled. I don't know which of us didn't want her to come out, maybe both. Finally exhaustion took hold, I was too tired to fight. She slipped into Auntie Lizzie's arms and I gave a cry of relief. Then when they laid her in my arms and I looked into her face, all crinkled and red from the exertion, I did cry. She was truly beautiful. I held her then, and I knew I couldn't give her up, not even to my own sister. I had agreed to let Iris raise her as a sister to her own baby, as twins. As I held her I knew that I had given away my right to her, but not my connection. I would always remember what happened; the awful act that had made her had not been completely erased, but I knew that every time I looked at her I would suffer a deeper pain, the regret of giving her away. I should have been grateful to Iris for being so willing to give my baby a home but that's not how it seemed to me then. If I could have looked forward to raising her, perhaps things would have been different. In that moment of looking into her newborn face, the only future I could see was wretched and painful. Auntie Lizzie's back was turned, just for a second.

To this day I don't exactly know what happened. I do and I don't. What I believe happened, I don't believe I could have done. She lay there in my arms as I stroked her face. She gave a muffled cry. She stopped moving. I screamed and dropped her to my lap. Auntie Lizzie came running but it was too late. She stared at the baby as she took it from me, saying over and over, 'Mary, Mother of Jesus, have mercy on this little soul.' In that moment I could hear nothing else. All I could feel was the pressure of my baby's head, still against my breast. All I could see was Auntie Lizzie's hand making the sign of the cross over that limp form slumped in her arms and hurriedly scooping a handful of water across its head.

During the days immediately afterwards, I had to force myself to look at Iris's baby, little Gayle. I hated her and I loved her. She was everything my own baby could have been. She was alive. I tried to be generous but I couldn't watch her nursing. My heart nearly heaved itself through my chest. It was so violent that I had to leave the room before it wrenched itself completely out of my body.

I walked a long way from the house to a place where I could sob and cry and punch the ground. My breasts ached. I ached. To feel my own child, to cradle her, to suckle her, to fall in to the pattern of nurturing and caring for my own little one as Iris was doing. The unfairness cut through me, and, most of all, the feeling that I had been punished by God for creating this life outside of marriage, and for all those times at the beginning when I wished it dead, and for the blackness deep inside myself.

Each day I had to sit in my room expressing milk to relieve the throbbing. The tears flooded out of me. This was worse than I'd ever anticipated. Even nature had conspired to support the judgement of Iris and Nell. Those two proper married ladies had their husbands and their social groups and their respectable ways, and Iris had the precious daughter I now longed for.

No one asked about the father. I didn't know him and I didn't want to, not after what he had done to me. I just wanted my baby back, and to care for her without interference. Mum would have come around, she didn't want to lose her grandchild. I needed some time to talk it through with her. She wasn't there for me when I needed her. Iris had got to her first; Iris and Nell didn't want the whole parish to know their sister had got in the family way without a husband to support her. They had never had to face the blackness that can make people do terrible things.

KATE

Mum puts down the receiver and takes an over-large shopping bag out of the linen cupboard in the hall.

'Maudie's taken a turn for the worse,' she says as she pulls clean underwear from a basket of freshly laundered clothes. Her movements are practised. She doesn't need to think about what to do. She knows exactly the few things that will be needed for the immediate trip.

'You can put your things in here, too,' she says. She checks the toiletry bag that is kept ready beside a bag of nighties in case she falls ill and has to be rushed to hospital. I remember the story she used to tell about her Uncle Tom. He was a single man who lived in a hotel despite being neither a smoker nor a drinker, and he didn't trust the other residents who indulged heavily in both. Tom lived in fear of waking in the middle of the night to the sound of fire sirens and crackling timber, so he kept all his possessions locked in a suitcase. Each night at bedtime he carefully packed his case and slid it under his bed where it could be grabbed quickly in an emergency. As Tom had anticipated, a fire did break out, but on the one night that he hadn't taken his usual precautions. He stood on the footpath across the street, dressed only in his pyjamas, and watched his few possessions go up in flames.

Jim, the Island's ambulance officer, knows where to find Mum's emergency bag, just in case.

We arrive in town on the two o'clock ferry. Uncle Vic is waiting in the pick-up and set-down zone outside the terminus. His fingers drum urgently on the steering wheel as I shove the shopping bag across the back seat and climb in beside it. Mum sits in the front with him.

'I dropped Phyll at the hospital on the way over,' he says as he starts the car. A woman steps off the kerb and stops on the roadway in front of us, waiting for traffic that's still some distance away. Uncle Vic sounds the horn and revs his engine impatiently at her for blocking his way. 'Some people!' he snorts.

The traffic through town is chaotic. It's not busy but drivers move in one direction, then change their minds and lane jump. For once I sympathise with Uncle Vic, then I close my eyes on the confusion and leave Mum to be his co-driver from the passenger seat. I know she will be silently driving the car, pressing her feet to the floorboards – brake, clutch, accelerate, brake – as is her habit whenever anyone else is in charge behind the wheel. She never complains or gives orders. She just silently wills them to do it her way. We are reversing into an angle park before Uncle Vic volunteers more information on Maudie.

'Another stroke – only a small one, mind you, but that's all it takes.' He gestures with his head towards a balcony some floors above us. 'Seems like Phyll and I have been living up there.'

Saint Phyll, I think and immediately chastise myself for

my meanness, but to Vic I say, 'You and Auntie Phyll have been terrific, Uncle Vic.' The frown between his eyebrows softens just a little. 'No problems, love. Families have to stick together.'

Another car pulls into the parking lot as we are walking up the steps to the hospital entrance. I hear someone call, 'Auntie Nell,' and turn to see Gayle waving from the passenger-side window. Uncle Vic waves back and begins to walk toward the car. Then he gives a funny little growl and turns on his heel, retreating to the hospital steps. Auntie Iris is so tiny in the back seat that I don't see her until I am right up close to the car. I guess that the man driving is Doug. Uncle Vic strides impatiently from one side of the steps to the other. The waistband of his shorts sits under the firm ball of his belly. For as long as I can remember, Uncle Vic has had a solid beer belly. More and more I think of him as a nut, a tough little nut.

Gayle introduces Doug just by name, without explaining who he is or why he is here. I can't help thinking that a deathbed is a strange place to choose to introduce your new boyfriend into your family. Gayle is displaying a strong sense of the unconventional in her middle age and Doug certainly fits the picture. His appearance stops just short of flash. One more button undone, one more piece of jewellery, one more centimetre on the freshly blow-dried hair and he would be a caricature. Luckily his in-built fashion barometer stops him just in time. We walk slowly back across the car park, letting Auntie Iris and Mum set the pace.

Usually Uncle Vic is the first one to shake a newcomer's hand and give them a welcoming slap on the back, but by the time we reach the steps he is skipping up the last few to swing the front door open for us. As Gayle calls out an introduction, he gives Doug a cursory nod and turns his attention back to Mum and Auntie Iris, who start to climb the steps, one behind the other, holding onto the railing. Doug moves to help Iris but Vic is there before him, taking her arm and propelling her gently upward.

'We're right, thanks,' he says gruffly.

I put my hand on the small of Mum's back and press gently, more for encouragement than for support. Gayle takes Doug's hand and they follow.

The knuckles on Maudie's hands are thick and lumpy from years of scrubbing pots and pans in the kitchens of the children's home. She was never a gentle person. Even walking through a doorway, Maudie would manage to crash into the jamb or catch her arm on the lock.

I am surprised at how small her face has become, as if she is shrinking away before our eyes. Her head is sup- ported on a stiff hospital pillow, surrounded by a circle of tight grey curls. Mum had organised a regular appointment for Maudie with the hairdressers who visited the nursing home. Every couple of months they would perm her hair, even when Maudie could no longer recognise any of her family and did not know that the figure staring back at her from the mirror was her own reflection.

Auntie Phyll rises from the chair next to the bed. She gathers up her knitting and her bag to move aside for Auntie Iris who, as the eldest of the close relatives, is the chief mourner. Uncle Vic gestures to Phyll to sit back down. He steers Iris to the other side and signals to me to bring a chair. It's awkward to squeeze one into the tight space, and with the drip and the bedside table, Auntie Iris won't be able to reach Maudie. Doug can see this too. He lifts the chair out of my hands and heads toward Phyll.

'Hello there,' he says in a voice that is at once cheerful and in control. 'I'm Doug, pleased to meet you. You don't mind if I move you along there, so all you ladies can fit in together? Good. Is that comfortable? I thought so. Iris, you can sit here. Do we have another chair for Nell? Us young ones can stand. Are you all comfortable? That's good.' In a few seconds he has the room organised, with Iris and Phyll sitting next to each other. Auntie Iris tentatively adjusts her position in the chair, as if unsure of how she came to be there. Phyll fans her flushed face vigorously with a magazine. A smiling Doug casually surveys the room. Uncle Vic grunts loudly and retreats to the far corner, where he folds his arms tightly, leans against the wall and pretends to look out of the window.

I look at Mum and Auntie Iris. This is one of those formal family occasions when we look to them to tell us the rules – what to do, when to speak, what to say. We are here to be with Maudie as she passes from one world to another. The Church tells us there is an afterlife. I know that Mum believes it, and Auntie Iris. Does Phyll, I wonder? Or Gayle? I think Gayle would want to believe, but what about Doug? It strikes me that Doug is a person who believes in the here and now. He's a man of action. He lives in the present. Maybe that's how Gayle has changed. She has swapped her limbo land for a life in the present. That's why she finds Doug so attractive. It's not his gold rings or the spill of hair from the front of his shirt, it's the immediacy, the sense of something happening. It's the passion for life that she and I talked about that day at the nursing home. I want to talk with Doug. I want to ask him where it springs from. The quietness in the room is intense.

A strange sound breaks the silence and stirs the mourners. Auntie Phyll sits in her chair, rocking backwards and forwards, one hand clutching at noises that, try as she might to stifle them, squeeze their way out. The hand that slips from her eyes is wet. She gulps for air and tries to speak. 'I just remembered . . . ' The shaking eases and she sighs deeply, wiping her eyes. 'I'm sorry,' she gasps, and pauses to take a deep breath. 'I just remembered the time Mum cleaned out Maudie's cupboard without telling her.'

Mum's face breaks into a smile and Phyll smiles too. I hope Iris will keep her equilibrium, but no. Her hand covers her mouth and she closes her eyes and a small trickle of wetness courses across her cheek. Gayle and I look at each other in the hope of finding some sense in the middle of this madness. Doug gives himself over to the humour of the situation and begins to laugh, although he cannot possibly know what is so funny about Nana cleaning out Maudie's wardrobe. Finally Mum recovers enough to speak. 'She went through Maudie's wardrobe and parcelled up clothes that Maudie hadn't used in years, and gave them to St Vincent de Paul without telling her. Next thing, Maudie comes home, thrilled with a shopping bag of dresses. She's been down to their op shop and bought all these things she loved, not realising they were her own clothes that Mum had given away.'

'It could only happen with Maudie,' says Phyll.

Iris sighs. 'She kept us amused, all right.'

I look at Maudie and wonder if she had found it amusing too. I once read something about strokes and how people could be paralysed and seemingly unconscious but completely functioning in their minds. They lie there, hearing and understanding everything, but unable to respond. Maybe Maudie can follow everything we say. I wonder how she feels about these revelations. Perhaps she is plotting a revenge that will take effect once she has passed over to the other side.

Iris has moved on to another anecdote, another Maudie story. 'One year she gave Bill the brightest red shirt with palm trees all over it,' she says.

'I got one of those, too,' Uncle Vic chuckles. 'Do you remember, Phyll?'

Auntie Phyll nods and laughs. 'Too right. I couldn't lose you in the middle of a crowded beach in that shirt.'

'I made the mistake of being polite. Said how nice it was. The next year I got two more.'

Doug hoots with enjoyment, and I wonder if it is at Maudie's eccentricity or the thought of Uncle Vic striding across the sand dressed in three gaudy red shirts.

'She obviously got a job lot,' says Mum.

'They were good shirts,' says Phyll, 'They took years to wear out.'

And that sets everyone off again.

Mum's quiet voice stops us. 'I think she's gone.'

I study Maudie's face against the pillow. She looks the same as when we walked into the room. Her head is nestled in a hollow on the pillow. Her hands lie outside the covers. Her eyes are closed. She is completely still. There is no rise and fall of her chest and from the heart monitor beside her bed comes one long drawn-out sound.

Gayle stirs first. Her voice eases into the atmosphere so that it is there before we realise she has spoken. 'Auntie Nell, why don't you lead us in a decade of the rosary.'

Mum's hand moves in the pocket of her skirt where her fingers have been quietly counting off prayer after prayer. That's the difference between Gayle and me. Where I avoid these things, she accepts that they matter to Mum and to

Auntie Iris. She accepts them and creates a space for them, where I want only to hide them. Mum's voice begins, 'The first decade of the Glorious Mystery, the Resurrection . . .'

GAYLE

It's dusk when we leave the hospital. I help Mum down the stairs and we sit on a seat near the entrance waiting for Doug to bring the car around. She's quite small beside me, even though I'm not a big person myself.

There's an orange-scented jessamine in flower in the front garden. I breathe in the sweet, heavy perfume and wonder what properties a New Age therapist would give it. Mum shuffles to get comfortable in the seat beside me.

'Well, there we are,' she says and sighs deeply. There is something so final in that release of air that for a moment I feel afraid to look sideways in case she has expired beside me. It's a great relief to feel her move again as she pulls her bag out from between us.

Her hands shake a little as she opens the clasp and takes out her hanky. It's already damp and creased. She dabs at the corners of her eyes and breathes deeply once more. 'It's a release,' she says. 'It's a release for all of us.'

There's something that reminds me of the way she was after Dad died. A deep sadness that is accompanied by acceptance. As if, despite her sorrow, she recognises that she and they had had a good innings and she shouldn't expect any more.

I've known for a while that I might not have her for much longer, but not because she's been ill. Mum's fit, despite her tiny appearance, and she's always had good health. It's just a feeling you get, knowing that, at her age, you need to spend as much time together as you can because it won't go on forever. I'd like to think that I'm prepared, but I know that losing her will hurt.

Doug has been talking about going on holidays. 'You've never been overseas,' he says, 'and I've only ever done that cruise ship thing. Why don't we take off somewhere?'

He comes home from the Mall with dozens of travel brochures and spreads them all over the table. Each week it's a new destination. I clear the table for meals and stack them in a bundle. After dinner we watch the travel shows on telly, with Doug making notes about the best times to visit, and the costs and who to travel with. I love the way he gets so excited and puts so much energy into it and I'd love to go, one day. Mum's early life toughened her up – I want these last years to be easy on her. If something happened while I was away, I couldn't forgive myself.

Doug pulls up at the grass verge and I help Mum to her feet. As we get into the car she says, 'Would you mind if I stayed the night at your place instead of going back to the home?'

'Of course, Mum,' I say. 'We can pick up some Chinese for tea.'

KATE

The soft click of bead on bead.

Outside the open window a family of flying foxes rustle about in the palm tree, loosening the baby coconuts. I roll onto my side, and as my eyes become accustomed to the dark I can make out her shape lying in the single bed on the other side of the room.

A car drives by. In that moment when its headlights lighten the room by only a couple of degrees, I see that she is lying on her back with her hands resting on her chest, counting off the beads in time with the prayer. Then, once again, I hear the sounds that woke me. A sniff. A wet moan. Quiet. I raise myself on one elbow, wondering what I can say.

I have only seen my mother cry once before, when my father died. That time I could put my arm around her and cry with her, letting her console me as I did her, sharing our grief and the sadness of losing the person who was central to our lives. This time I feel no pain. It doesn't matter that she was rare, Maudie has ended up as a bit player in my life, an eccentric, a character. She added colour and humour but she was not crucial. My tomorrow will not feel empty because Maudie has gone. I came here to mark her passing because it was requested of me. I do my duty and I also feel sadness, but my role this time is to support and I cannot find it in me to mourn deeply. In my eyes Maudie didn't have a life. She hasn't lost anything. Perhaps things will even be better for her now.

A low sob brings me back to my immediate concern. How can I console my mother?

The shaggy nylon mat is warm and scratchy against my feet. I slide it across the floor with me. I kneel next to her bed and put an arm across her body.

'Did I wake you?' Her voice is thick with tears.

'Are you okay?'

'It's just accepting it, that's all.' The beads clink again in her hands. 'She's the first of us to go.'

'Don't you get any ideas about following.' I wrap my arms around her frail body, one resting on the pillow around her head and one over her, and I lay my head on her shoulder.

'Was Maudie always strange?'

'Not when she was young, apart from the fits.'

I remember Maudie sitting on the back steps of our

house, playing with me, acting the goat. She stops. Her eyes glaze over for a minute. Then she turns and vomits through the steps into the drain that carries the water from the grease trap out into the garden. I am embarrassed more than surprised. Maudie does strange things but vomiting is a sign of illness. She sees me staring at her and wipes her mouth with a crumpled handkerchief. 'Tell your mother I need some molasses,' she says.

Mum suddenly pats my arm as if it is she consoling me, not I her. 'She was seven when they started. Iris and I were playing with her. Right there in front of my eyes, she started to jerk about and her eyelids fluttered a bit. Then she started frothing, not a lot, just a trace of white foam. Your nana came running and pushed her fingers into Maudie's mouth and this thin line of spittle trailed out. A convulsion, the doctor called it. They didn't know too much about epilepsy then. She could run about with us, then all of a sudden her eyes would grow distant and the spasm would pass right through her. A moment later her eyes would turn to you with no memory of what had just happened.'

'That's not enough to explain why she was so eccentric.'

'Well, it meant she didn't have an ordinary upbringing. She needed to be looked after.'

'Did Nana protect her?'

'She worried Maudie would have a fit on the bus or come to harm. If she seemed tired, she wasn't allowed to go to school. Poor Maudie, she didn't get much of an education, and nor did I for a while.'

'You stayed at home to look after her?'

'Someone had to. Nana had to work and so did Iris. We had no father supporting us.'

'So you played mother.'

'Nana never faltered as a mother. She was always concerned about our welfare. But Maudie needed constant looking after. She never really learned to do things for herself. After Nana died, she just didn't have a clue about running the house and paying the bills and caring for herself.' Mum seemed almost calm again. She slipped one hand over mine and patted it.

'The dementia came on slowly. At first she'd lose things or she wouldn't recognise people, then she stopped caring for herself. I'd take her to stay with me so I could give her a bath and wash her hair, but I couldn't keep up with it. She was heavy. I couldn't lift her. And she was a devil for leaving the gas stove on. I was worried she would burn the house down around us. That's when we found her the place in the home.'

I could feel the muscles of her face screwing up to hold back another burst of tears. 'It's going to be very lonely,' she cried out. 'I've had to look out for her for so long and now she's gone.'

I think to myself, Maudie has needed you even after your own children grew up and moved away. I want to say, Don't worry. I'll always need you. Even when I run away from you, I need you. I need you always to be here. I need to know that this part of my life stays the same, that you will always be here for me when I choose to come back.

'She was eighty last birthday, and I know at eighty you can't last forever.' The sobs begin to choke back the words but she presses on. 'It's only a matter of time now before I end up in the home too. I can't keep managing the house. It's getting too much for me and all of you are so far away. None of you come home often enough to warrant keeping such a big place. I'll have to give it up.'

I want to promise her I'll come home more often. She won't be alone. I'll help her manage. It's not lies but I know that anything I do will have to be from a distance. Coming back here to live is not an option. I don't want it. Dan doesn't want it. And most importantly, I know that deep down she doesn't want it either. Instead of speaking, I hug her tighter and pat her hair and press my face into the softness of her sunken cheek.

The next morning begins in the same way as every other morning I have spent in this house. At six o'clock there's a rustling and a creaking as Uncle Vic rolls his belly to the side of the bed and swings his legs to the floor. I've never seen this happen but the sounds are the same as the ones my dad used to make when he got up at six o'clock, and, just like Dad used to, Uncle Vic wanders out to the kitchen and switches on the electric kettle.

I slide down the mattress, pulling the sheet around me to keep out the early morning coolness. In the bed opposite, Mum is sleeping restfully after the release of last night's tears. Her snores are as familiar as Vic's tea-making. There's a moderate snuffling sort of drawback, followed by a pause and then a long tuneful whistle. When we were kids, we used to eavesdrop on Mum and Dad's Sunday afternoon nap and laugh ourselves silly at the sound of Dad's deep drawback followed by Mum's responding whistle. It's satisfying to know that all these years after losing Dad, Mum has taken up his part in this domestic operetta.

Beyond the snores are the reassuring noises of Uncle Vic making bread-and-butter sandwiches, and as I lie with my eyes closed I remember the familiar taste of freshly buttered bread, folded over and dunked in steaming hot tea. I listen for the soft chink and scrape of a teacup being set down quietly on the bedside table. At this end of the morning there's no need for small talk.

The appointment with the undertakers is set for eleven o'clock, so there's no need to rush. I offer to iron Mum's dress and as I do I see the fraying and thinning that her weary old eyes, shaded by cataracts, can no longer pick up. While I wait to use the shower, I escape downstairs to where Vic is busy hosing down the cement floor.

The under-the-house is separated into squares by the cement house posts. Next to each post is a huge tub overflowing with fishtail ferns of all varieties, and to one side is a tiered metal stand displaying a collection of ornamental pot plants. Droplets of water hang from every leaf and the air is cool against my skin. I shiver with the unexpectedness of it. Uncle Vic has moved outside and is hosing the plastic garden furniture in the backyard.

The buffalo grass is broad-leaved and firm. Dad wouldn't have it in his lawn. 'Not worth the trouble,' he said. 'One dry spell and your lawn's dead.' He planted blue couch and nurtured it like a baby. On Saturdays he'd drag out an old sugar bag and his lawn tools and spend a couple of hours listening to the football on the radio as he painstakingly dug nut grass from his prized lawn. Our front yard looked like a bowling green. During the annual drought, the lawn shrivelled till only the threadlike backbone of the runners could be seen. Sure enough, every time, with the rain, Dad's lawn came back, good as new, a thickly matted carpet that your feet sank into, and when you stood back and gazed onto this perfectly even surface, you were amazed by its definite tinge of blue.

I help Uncle Vic bring in the chairs. The water drips onto my legs and runs down and across my bare feet. It's not often that I go without shoes. I hardly feel the earth at all these days.

'You should stand on the grass more often,' says Uncle

Vic. I look at the lawn and my confusion must show on my face. 'In bare feet,' he says. 'Once a day.'

He gives a little chuckle and tweaks the hose spray in the direction of my toes. 'To ground yourself,' he says. 'On the ground. Release the static electricity.'

I give a startled jump at the thought of it.

'Think about it,' says Uncle Vic. 'It makes sense. We go about in cars and buses, touching metal and using energy. It's only natural the body builds up static electricity. We never ground ourselves. If you were an electricity circuit in a house, you'd have to be grounded. We should do it for our bodies, too.'

I step outside again. The thick blades of grass are strong against my feet. I roll and rub them sideways and feel a small tingle. I don't know if it's the static electricity but it feels good. Uncle Vic is right. My garden is an inner-city balcony. It's not often that I get to feel grass and press the soles of my feet into fresh earth. It's a long time since I stretched my toes this wide and felt the scratching and rubbing and the sense of aliveness.

'There's nothing like a cold shower to remind you how it feels to be alive.' Phyll patters out of the bathroom. Her bare feet make squeaking noises on the linoleum.

'I don't know how you do it, Auntie Phyll.'

'It's one of Vic's ideas. He says it improves the circulation.'

I volunteer to let Mum shower first.

'That's generous of you,' she says.

'Not really. Once I get in, I want to stay for as long as I like.'

'You'll be lucky,' Phyll calls from the kitchen. 'The hot water will have definitely run out by then.'

In the kitchen Phyll is arranging individual packets of breakfast cereal in a basket. She has coffee and teapots ready to make both. Bacon is sizzling in a pan. 'I thought I'd fry the eggs this morning,' she says.

I would like to ask if she and Vic eat like this every day but decide that she might take it as a criticism. Instead I carry the basket of cereal into the dining room.

Photos of their sons and grandchildren are nestled in amongst the postcards and fishing trophies on the dresser. They're family photos: group shots taken at shopping centres in the different suburbs around the country where their sons now live. The boys' faces are familiar, all having a resemblance of one sort or another to Uncle Vic. Peter has his nose, Brendan the cleft in his chin, Paul a certain look around his eyes. The women are all different. One has short brown hair and another is bleached blonde. I can't imagine how Phyll can feel close to these strangers and I wonder what it is like to see flashes of yourself reflected back at you by your own child growing up.

'Auntie Phyll?'

She is running her hand under the cold-water tap. Her face is scrunched in pain. 'I should know better than to leave the fork sitting on a hot pan,' she says. 'Especially one that hot.' She takes a deep breath and holds it in an effort to make the pain abate.

I look over her shoulder. She smells of lemons. Ripe cut lemons. It's an invigorating scent. Her hand has a red mark across the palm. She holds herself tightly by the wrist. 'Vic has some of that aloe vera stuff in the bathroom cupboard,' she says. 'Get it for me, will you?'

Mum is towelling herself dry when I knock on the door. She opens the door a fraction and passes the tube of gel to me. I take it back to the kitchen and squeeze some onto Phyll's palm, smearing it lightly over the red weal.

'Auntie Phyll, have you ever wished you had a daughter?' I ask. She winces. Her eyes fill with tears. 'I've hurt you,' I say. She sucks in a breath and holds it. Her body is tight, her shoulders clenched, and the grip that one hand has on the wrist of the other is tight enough to strangle it. 'I'm sorry.' The words escape my lips in a whisper. The tears spill down her cheeks. How could the burn cause so much pain?

Vic walks in the back door. 'Where's my suit?' he says.

Phyll pushes me aside. 'Where do you think?' she says as she rushes through to her bedroom.

Vic glares at me. 'What have you done?' he demands angrily as he follows her and slams the door.

IRIS

Gayle drives me to the undertaker's and Phyll and Iris meet us there. We use Thornton's. They've done the right thing by us before, when Bill and Jack died. They're very respectful and it doesn't take long to choose a reasonably priced casket and one mourning car.

For the service, we chose the parish church near the nursing home. I know the priests there because they come up to our chapel every morning to say Mass for the elderly people. It's not far from Nell's old place, and Gayle and Noel used to be in the parish, too. Father Keenan meets us at the door of the presbytery and sees us into the office. It's a bit crowded with all of us, so Vic and Gayle and Katey wait outside in the grounds. We all agree on a Requiem Mass and the details are pretty straightforward, but then Phyll gets nervous about saying yes without Vic there beside her.

'I don't see what the problem is,' I tell her. 'If it's the cost you're worried about, that's all in the funeral home. And if we want to change that, we'll have to go back, but let's clear up here first and let Father get on with his business.'

Nell's the clever one where people are concerned. She's not impatient like me. Finally she interrupts us. 'Let's get Vic in and run it past him before we give the okay.' Well, Father's very good and goes over everything again, and Vic nods agreement and it's all sorted out in two seconds. I'm not sure whether Phyll looks relieved or exhausted, the way she's slumped in that uncomfortable office chair.

By the time we're finished I'm dying for a cup of tea. I can't go for long these days without a bit of refreshment. My energy sags easily and I need a quick pick-me-up; just a cup of tea and a biscuit does the trick. Gayle offers to drive us to the Mall nearby while Vic takes Phyll home.

We stop at the coffee shop near the big haberdashery. Nell and I squeeze onto the soft, cushioned bench seat. Gayle takes out her reading glasses and studies the menu, though why I don't know since she chooses an iced coffee just like always.

'We'll have to put an announcement in the paper,' I say, and fish about in my bag for a biro and a piece of paper to write it out on.

'Death or funeral?' asks Gayle.

'Both,' says Nell.

'Does anyone ever read those things?' asks Katey. Well, you can tell that girl leads a strange life, but I suppose in the big city people don't know each other like we do here.

'Hatches, matches and dispatches,' laughs Gayle. 'Never know when I might come across my own.' She takes the paper and the pen and pushes her glasses up the bridge of her nose. For a moment I see myself doing the same thing. It's a strange feeling I get at times with Gayle. It's only ever with little things and only occasionally – I recognise my own habits, or sometimes Mum's. You'd think they got handed down with the hair colour or the height.

'There's a lot of people who might like to come to the funeral,' says Nell. 'One of the nurses at the hospital came up to me the other night to offer her condolences because she'd heard about Maudie.' She turns to young Kate. 'You don't realise how highly regarded she was.'

'If Maudie had such a satisfying and complete life then why was she always so angry and frustrated?' Kate says back.

Well, I could sense Nell's hackles go up then. 'Where do you get these ideas from?' she says. 'Maudie wasn't like that all the time.'

'More often than not,' I say. 'I know how you feel about this, Nell, but it's true that Maudie got left behind in Mum's wake.'

Gayle takes off her reading glasses and shoves them back into the case. 'One day I went around to the house to visit Nana and she started telling me a story about how the man in the corner house gave her a wolf whistle as they were walking home that day from the bus stop. The poor man was only doing it for a joke and Nana gave him a cheeky response. She didn't think of Maudie at all and just assumed he meant it for herself. Maudie flew off the handle and stormed on home. She was still stewing about it when I got there.'

Nell looks down at her skirt and smooths the thin

paper napkin over her lap. 'Maudie never could control that temper of hers,' she says.

Well, that set me off. I know I was tired and irritated with Phyll for holding up the proceedings that morning and then getting Vic involved for no good reason in what should have been kept between the three of us. But Nell's always carried on as if Mum was the perfect mother when you could see plain as day that Maudie didn't get a fair run. 'The point is, Nell, that Mum was just so used to having all the attention outside the family, she couldn't see Maudie as anything other than a child. You and I and Phyll, we had our weddings and our husbands and families. Mum could see that and she deferred to it, but Maudie was always there and Mum could never come to see her as separate.'

'I don't recall things being like that.' When Nell is challenged her voice gets thin and high, and it's always a sign that she's putting on her stubborn coat. I seem forceful from the outside but Nell can just put up brick walls and sit behind them. And one of her walls is to do with Maudie and Mum. It just makes me want to knock them down.

'After you and Jack bought that place out on the estate, you weren't around so much to notice what was happening,' I say, 'but Bill and I lived close by and I saw more of them than you did. Mum didn't mean any harm but sometimes Maudie got left in the background. No wonder she ended up feeling frustrated and overlooked.'

And that's the end of it as far as I'm concerned. I put my

cup down and open my purse to pay but Gayle tells me to put it away. Then Nell insists on giving Gayle a $20 note to cover the bill and she pats me on the hand and says, 'Don't you two hang about here on our account. We can catch the bus.' That's how I knew she was still cross, not letting Gayle drive her back to Phyll's.

KATE

'Do you have a black outfit to wear to the funeral?' I ask Mum as we wander out into the shopping aisles.

'I don't bother with that rubbish. It's a funeral, not a fashion parade,' she says tersely, but I know it's to do with her argument with Auntie Iris, not with me. I've never known them to have cross words before, so I can only think that it's a reaction to all the stress of Maudie's illness and death. I remember Phyll's outburst only this morning and think that perhaps it has worn everyone down more than I realised.

'Did you have something in mind to wear?' I slip the words out carefully.

'I could do with a new dress.'

We wander into a chain store where there is row after

row of patterned and plain dresses in all colours and styles suitable for older ladies. It's been one of Mum's favourite dress shops for years.

'I need a size fourteen around my middle now, she says, 'but I'm still only size ten across the shoulders.'

'Should we look at dresses or matching skirts and tops?'

Mum goes in search of the shop assistant to see if they will split up the sizes and I wander over to the more expensive rack toward the back of the shop. These are more tailored outfits in better fabrics and with more attention to detail.

'I should have known I'd find you here,' says Mum. 'There's no point us looking there. I'm not paying those prices for clothes.'

'But look at the quality.' I point out the stitching and the fall of the fabric and the way it is cut to match the pattern printed on the material. Mum may not want to pay these prices but she appreciates good workmanship. 'What if we went halves and that would take care of your birthday present this year?'

Mum hesitates and feels the softness of the material.

'It would save me mailing something later,' I say.

She doesn't say yes, but she doesn't say no either. She moves down the rack to another outfit in the same style but a different colour. She allows me to hold it up against her as she studies it in the full-length mirror, and pauses

again to note the details on the price ticket. 'No harm in trying it on,' she says.

In the changing room I help her peel off her dress and
she stands in her petticoat and singlet waiting for me to
unhook the new outfit from its hanger. She leans against
my shoulder as I crouch down and hold the waistband of
the skirt open for her to step into it.

'I have a hard time touching my toes these days.'

'We'll get you doing tummy crunches every morning.'

'Oh yeah!' she says, and with relief I register the lighter
tone that has crept into her voice.

She pulls the top down over her head and smooths the
wide, lace-trimmed collar and straightens her back to stand
taller. She smiles, and when she does her face glows and
she seems ten years younger.

'Go on, Mum,' I say, 'you deserve a little spoiling now
and again.'

We sit in the same church we used to come to every Sunday.
It looks exactly the way it was then, a long, low, colonnaded
building of pale bricks with an expansive vaulted ceiling. It
has the grandeur of a cathedral mixed with the clean, plain
lines of a seventies church planned for young families and
folk Masses with hymns sung to the strumming of guitars. It
was designed to catch the faintest of breezes, and even on
a hot day the air inside is fresh.

This is not the church that Maudie came to. She lived in

a different parish, an old parish where the congregation was dying or moving away, leaving its graceful old church empty of people and of song. We lived in a new suburb in a new house and came to this new church. Dad was an early riser, so we were dragged out of bed for six o'clock Mass, and he always liked to sit in one of the back pews. For the communion procession we lined up in the aisle like a string of ducklings out for a walk with their parents.

Mum sits in the front pew between Auntie Iris and Auntie Phyll. Iris is straight. She's bony and small, like a little bird. She reminds me of Nana. Phyll is still plump in a middle-aged, lumpy way. It strikes me that it is harder for people to grow older gracefully in the tropics. At least it seems that way when I look at some of the older people I know. Their skin grows blotchy from exposure to the sun and their clothes never seem to fit well.

Mum sits slightly stooped. Her bottom spreads out along the seat. I think of her dressing this morning, standing in the bedroom in her singlet and panties. I think of the way she wears her bra over the top of her singlet. Her body is all bent and knobbly, with only her middle solid and round. She reminds me of those drawings of elves in old children's books, all big round bellies with thin, bony legs. She always used to be thin, thin wrists and arms and ankles. I used to hate her boniness, the wrinkles on her arms and hands, all the little telltale signs of her age, but this morning when I saw her bent frame and muscles sagging on her skinny thighs, I wanted to wrap her in my arms and cradle her like a baby.

No, not like a baby. That's the contradiction. I'm her baby. I wanted to hold her the way I used to hold the edge of her skirt, to stop her from leaving me. I can feel her gradually leaving me. She's not slipping away but going from choice, slowly easing herself away from the world. It frightens me to see how easily she can leave me behind. What would I do without her? What an irony! After all these years of pushing her away, of wanting and not wanting her, it's she who can walk away from me. I've been so concerned with escaping from the closeness of her that I haven't considered the possibility of losing her altogether. There's always been the four of them, a brick wall of sisters holding back the inevitable, but Maudie's death has broken the spell.

The hand on my shoulder is Gayle's. She doesn't understand. She sees my tears as sadness at losing Maudie. We haven't talked about these things. I suppose I am sad that Maudie died but I have to admit I was irritated that her life was so wasted, waiting for nothing, existing to be her mother's companion.

Mum sees it differently of course. She says I don't understand. Nana only had Maudie's best interests at heart. She wanted Maudie to be safe. Mum says that you can't judge yesterday by the way things are today. Maybe she's right.

The family file into the pews at the front of the church behind Mum and Iris and Phyll. It has been a long time since I have seen some of my cousins and this is the first time I've met their children and partners. Brendan is unmistakable, sitting next to Vic and mimicking his father's profile. I guess that the woman beside him is his wife, though I lose track of who is married and to whom and with what children as a result. Gayle joins Uncle Vic and me in the second row. Doug is with her and I feel Uncle Vic bristle as Doug sits down. I can almost hear the word 'interloper' escape on a breath. A young woman, more like a girl, taps Gayle on the shoulder. Gayle turns and they exchange a few hurried words. She turns back and sees me looking. 'Simone,' she mouths. Brent's girlfriend, and I guess that the baby screaming at the back of the church is theirs. It takes a funeral to bring families closer. Though neither of my brothers can make it, somehow I think their absences are more easily forgiven than mine would have been.

The Priest appears from behind the altar. He walks forward to speak to the senior undertaker. Then he continues down to the front pew where he has a quick word with Iris and Mum and Phyll.

The funeral service is short. There are no eulogies for Maudie. What can you say about a life half lived? And who would say them? There was no one who was close to Maudie. She seemed only to know people second-hand, through her mother or her sisters. There are prayers and a few words from the Priest about how religious she was and I think to myself, She didn't have the opportunity to be otherwise. The whole procedure takes much longer because they have a full Mass as well. That's Mum's doing.

GAYLE

Noel and I got married in this church. The boys were baptised here, too. And every Sunday for nearly twenty-seven years we came here for Mass.

I wish I could say this place gave me comfort but that isn't the case. I can't claim to have felt the black depression that other people suffer. Maybe if I had, I would have turned to the Church, but I just felt a slow compression of my soul and the Church couldn't help fix that. To my mind, religion was part of what oppressed me, part of the rules that hemmed in my life.

Noel was a churchgoing man. He truly believed in those religious ideals about the good Catholic family praying together and staying together. We just didn't share those ideals, or much else. It takes more than a Nuptial Mass to make a marriage. I tried to live up to his expectations, until I realised it was more important for me to live up to mine.

We have these conventions, the Baptism, the Nuptial Mass, the Requiem. I go along with them for Mum's sake, Mum's and Auntie Nell's. They've used these customs to mark out their lives and they're too old to change now. I knew it would be important for them to choose a Requiem for Maudie because it wouldn't be proper to send her off with anything less.

It's surprising to see so many people here today, more than the family friends that were expected. Mum sits back on the seat in front of me and I kneel forward so I can whisper to her. 'Do you know who those people are?'

Auntie Nell turns around as Mum shrugs her shoulders. 'Probably to do with the children's home,' she whispers back. 'You'd be surprised how many people still remember her.'

The children's home was a sad place, tucked in under the shadow of the hill around the back of the town. There were three buildings set at angles to one another, like spokes of a partly constructed wheel, and joining at the front office. It sat, desolate-looking, at the end of a long drive and surrounded by a bare expanse of cut grass. We always used to pass it at dusk on our way home from Sunday afternoon drives out along the Cape, so we never saw children playing out there and the only sign of life was the fringe of harsh electric light that escaped around the edges of the curtains. When Mum was at her wits' end with us, she would say, 'I'll send you to the children's home,' and the threat was enough to restore order quick smart. I never associated the place with Maudie. To me it was the place where bad children were sent to be punished.

When the boys were young, Maudie used to visit us every week on her day off. Nana told me not to let her be a nuisance, but she was never that. She'd arrive in time for lunch, and when the littlies went down for an afternoon nap she'd keep me company while I did the ironing. We'd sit under the house hoping to catch whatever breeze there was. She was a funny old thing. No matter what the weather – it could be the hottest day on record or the wettest day in months – she wouldn't complain. People could really set her off, but the things that would annoy most of us she just let pass her right by.

We'd sit down there under the house and chat away, Maudie and I, but I could tell she wasn't really interested in our conversation. She was filling in time until the boys woke up, or, later, until they came home from school. She was in her element with the kids and they loved her. I can't really describe what it was that Maudie did with the boys. It was truly a gift, like she was one of them but grown up at the same time. She was never too tired to talk or play or listen or read another story. And she kept them in line.

The boys used to bring their friends home, so we often had six or eight children riding their bikes in the driveway, playing games in the backyard, or doing quieter things inside. It didn't matter what was happening, Maudie was in the middle of it.

As the boys grew older, they still seemed to keep their attachment to her. Brent would go and see her in the nursing home, even when she didn't know him any more. He has a sentimental streak, but I like to think it was because of the genuine interest she took in him when he was a kid.

One day my neighbour Trish stopped by. Her Paulie was the same age as my Chris and in the same class up at the convent school. Normally Trish was a chirpy sort of person, but on this afternoon she seemed subdued as we sat in the dining room and talked about the P&T meeting that was coming up. As she talked she stared out the window at Maudie playing with the children in the yard below.

'Miss Maud is just the way I remember her,' she said, interrupting the discussion. It was a complete surprise to me, since I didn't know she had come across Maudie before and I was not used to hearing Maudie referred to as Miss anything. She was always just Maudie. I didn't know what to say, and as if in response to my quiet, Trish turned and said, 'My dad died when I was eight and for a while Mum just couldn't cope. My brothers went out to my uncle, where they could make themselves useful on the farm. Out there, every pair of hands counts. My sister and I were sent to the children's home. It was tough, especially when they separated us.' She fiddled with a button on the front of her jacket. 'My sister was four years older than me and they had rules about the age groups in each dormitory. They didn't ever change the rules for anyone.' The button threatened to come off. 'It was hard,' she said, 'really hard. But Miss Maud was terrific with us kids. She made us feel like someone cared.'

I had always thought about Maudie as belonging to us. That was the first time I saw that she had something else, something away from the family.

KATE

Mum and Iris and Phyll stand at the front door of the church. Old friends and acquaintances stop to shake hands and offer condolences. Outside, people huddle in twos and threes in the sparse shade of the bottlebrush trees and chat about inconsequential things. It's mostly family and old friends who have attended.

Uncle Vic organises the pallbearers. They carry the coffin to the hearse and slide it in along the shiny chrome rungs. The undertaker's assistants stand about like bodyguards waiting for instructions to move.

'Do you want to come in our car?' Gayle is at my side,

nudging my elbow. 'There's only Doug and me, we've got plenty of room.'

I came to the church in the mourning car with Mum and Iris and Phyll, but it seems more appropriate to leave them to travel to the cemetery alone. Selfishly, I think Gayle and Doug might be more light-hearted company for this ride and it will be more comfortable in the back of the Falcon than squashed up in Uncle Vic's ancient Corolla.

Doug leaves us to wait at the front of the church while he collects the car from the parking lot at the back.

'Do you know many of the people here?' I ask.

'The odd one. Not many.' Gayle surveys the small group at the church door. 'They're mostly old-timers from the south side, and some people Maudie knew through the church or through work.'

'Did Maudie ever sing you to sleep when she visited?'

'The way Maudie sang, I did my best to be asleep already,' she laughs. 'Poor old Maudie. In some ways it wasn't much of a life, was it?' After days of listening to platitudes, it is a relief to know that someone shares my opinion of Maudie's wasted life. The face Gayle pulls makes me laugh. She stretches out her hand and touches my arm. 'I'm glad you didn't go the same way.' The squeeze on my arm is soft.

'What do you mean?' I want to hear her say it, aloud.

'You were such a quiet kid, a bit of a loner, and Auntie

Nell was always so protective. I thought you might never leave home, never make a life of your own.'

'There were times when that seemed like the easiest option.'

'Well, the easiest option isn't always the best, and in your case you're certainly better off for taking the risk. What prompted you to make the break?'

'I felt suffocated. I needed to get away. I didn't want to be like Maudie. I know it sounds cruel but I wanted to be more in life than just company for my ageing mother.'

Gayle twists sideways in her seat and turns her head to look at me. 'Our mothers are wonderful in their own way, Kate, but they're not above a bit of emotional blackmail when they're feeling lonely and miserable.'

'Does Auntie Iris do that to you too?'

'You bet,' says Gayle. 'I sometimes think they had daughters as a cushion against old age. What's worse is, I'm beginning to wish I had had one myself.'

Gayle and I laugh in unison. 'I can't complain. My sons have chosen lovely girls but the old proverb never lies: "A son is a son till he marries a wife but a daughter is a daughter for the whole of her life."'

Doug pulls up at the kerb and waits. Mum and Iris and Phyll are getting into the mourning car and I go up to it and lean in the open door. 'Gayle's giving me a lift to the cemetery,' I say, 'I'll see you there.' Auntie Phyll makes another joke about Maudie giving them a limousine ride and where's the champagne. The black-suited assistant shuts the door firmly and their car slips down the drive to join the hearse. Doug has the engine going as I climb into his car and we roll off with the rest of the cortege. I notice that we are first in line after the mourning car.

'Do you think we should let Uncle Vic go in front?'

'Is there a protocol with the cortege?' says Doug.

'I think there's a protocol with Uncle Vic,' I suggest. 'He can get a bit touchy about his position in the family – oldest surviving male and all that.'

'We're on our way now,' says Gayle. 'Too late to change.'

Doug turns on the radio just enough to hear it inside the car. It's a local radio station that plays golden oldies.

'Just like us, eh darl.' He slaps Gayle lightly on the knee. 'Get on your dancing shoes.'

'It wouldn't be proper, Douggie,' she says. 'We're on our way to a funeral.'

'Interment, darl. We've done the funeral.' Doug has a seat cover made of polished round balls that is meant to massage your back as you drive along and stop the sweat from gathering around your rear end. I watch him move about in his seat, unsure whether he's giving himself a back massage or whether the cover is just uncomfortable.

I undo the seatbelt and slide over behind Doug so I can talk to Gayle without forcing her to twist around to look over her shoulder.

'Did you ever see much of Uncle Vic and Auntie Phyll when you were growing up?' I ask.

'I can't remember anything in particular. I used to see the boys at Nana's but they were a fair bit younger than I was and they were boys. I knew your brothers better, even though we didn't have a lot in common. Auntie Nell says Gerry's job takes him travelling a lot.'

'He's marketing manager for South-East Asia. He's always off somewhere or other. I never get to see him.'

Doug lets out a burst of laughter. 'So we're selling stuff back to them now, are we? Is it knick-knacks and furry animals?'

'Nothing so cuddlesome, Doug. It's combine harvesters and heavy machinery.'

He looks at me through the rear-vision mirror, his cheeks dotted red with good humour. In a funny way he reminds me of Uncle Vic.

'I remember Sunday mornings at Nana's,' I say, trying to bring the conversation back to the family. 'Morning tea after Mass.'

'Maudie would come in from Mass and put on the religious service on television and *Songs Of Praise* on the radio. You couldn't get away from it.'

'Except when she got angry with Nana and swept the floor. Then you couldn't hear anything above the banging of the broom on the door jambs and skirting boards.'

'Dad hated taking her anywhere in the car. She used to

bang the door so hard the whole car shook. He thought she would tear it off its hinges.'

Doug gives up trying to follow us and fixes his eyes on the cortege in front. This is as good a time as any to ask difficult questions. 'Was there something that happened at some point in the family, some big issue or a disgrace?'

Gayle thinks for a moment before replying. 'I think there might have been a falling out at some time between Mum and Phyll.' She pauses as she thinks again. 'I know Dad and Uncle Vic didn't get along. They weren't invited to my wedding, but that was just Dad being jealous. He didn't get along with anybody.' She shrugs her shoulders. 'We didn't go to any of their family celebrations, come to think of it, but I didn't know any of the boys really.'

Doug turns the radio off. Our jovial mood has fallen into reverie and the funereal spirit of the day overtakes us. As we turn into the gates of the old cemetery down near the bay, he turns to us and says, 'Has Phyll always had that awful habit of scratching?'

When the old cemetery was in West End, near St Mary's, this place was called the new cemetery. It's getting full now, Mum told me the other day. There's another one, a big one that's opened up out past the university. That makes this one the old cemetery now.

The last time I came here was to bury my father. The place is smaller than I remember and now, thinking of the sadness in my mother's voice when she told me about the new cemetery, I wonder if closing this one means she will miss out on being buried with him. They spent so many happy years together. All those romantic notions about love and marriage were their reality, as they lived out their marriage vows. What an awful dilemma for her, to feel torn between life and lying in everlasting peace with your soulmate. No wonder she seems sad at times.

The cortege travels slowly down the narrow streets of the cemetery until the hearse comes to a stop. I have no idea how they manage to find the right plot. To me it has always seemed a jumble of tombs and monuments.

'They're burying her with Nana,' says Gayle, nodding toward a place in the middle of the row of graves. There's a mound of freshly dug soil heaped to one side and the rectangular space it has come from is roped off with thick shiny black cord slung between short chrome supports. The Priest is already standing there in his purple and white garments.

Gayle and I help Mum and Iris from the mourning car and along the path to the grave. Doug brings up the rear, taking Phyll by the elbow. Next thing, Vic appears on Phyll's other side and, sweeping his arm around her, he dislodges Doug's hand and pushes her on ahead with the others. The three sisters group themselves to one side of the Priest. I stand next to Mum, holding her arm to help her balance on the uneven ground. Phyll wipes her nose with the back of her hand. Vic tugs an oversized hanky from his pocket and hands it to her. The other mourners are scattered around the gravesite, heads bowed. The sun beats down strongly on the back of my head. Father Keenan's words drone on and I feel myself drifting off. High above us a bird scoops and crests on the wind, which carries it just a couple of kilometres across to the Town Common, where it probably has a nest in the nature reserve. A breeze flows in lightly from the bay, bringing with it the smell of salt and muddy mangrove flat which, combined with the strength of the sun, makes me feel nauseous. Mum leans her weight on my arm as the heat begins to affect her. I move to shade her from the direct sun and put an arm around her for balance. I can feel her slipping and I can't hold her. I can only control her downward movement and help her land as softly as possible on a mound of dirt.

Immediately the assistant is there with a flask of water and someone is fanning her with the handout from the Mass. Vic helps us back to the mourning car where the driver has opened the windows to let the air flow through. Mum says she feels better. The colour slowly returns to her face and she wipes the sweat beads from her upper lip with a linen handkerchief.

I walk over to the shade of a tree next to the tombstones near to the car and read one of the inscriptions. 'Mary O'Donnell, wife and mother, born 1883, died 1938.'

This cemetery has been the main burying ground for most of the life of this town. It has taken the bones of pioneers, old settlers, and generations of townsfolk, turning them to dust on this curve of the bay, next to the nature reserve where the native birds nest. I go back to the car and lean in the window.

'Where's Dad's grave?'

'Further down, next to his parents.' Then Mum points in the opposite direction. 'And Mum's sister Auntie Maggie is buried down there, about three rows away from Mum.' She is about to tell me about a few others but I straighten up and move off in the original direction she pointed. I stay on the pathways, remembering some forgotten person's voice at my ear warning me that it's disrespectful to walk on graves.

The plot is a big one. There's Dad and his parents and his unmarried brother. Unmarried people always seem to be buried with their parents, like Maudie with Nana. Is it so they won't be lonely? The conventions are amusing. I remember Uncle Frank. Mum said he was injured in the war, in the head, and he lived with us for a while when I was little. He and Maudie would have made a good couple. There's a photo under glass on Dad's tombstone. Mum must have had it done without telling us. It's a photo from our last holiday together. His hair is thin and white and his face has fallen into jowls. Behind the lines and the sunken eyes there's a trace of the bright young man from his wedding photo. I used to think I looked like Dad but lately I have grown much more like Mum. It's in the line of the nose and the way the cheeks slip downwards, exposing the shape of the bones, and my body shape has grown more like hers.

I wander back towards the burial service, searching for Auntie Maggie's grave. I don't really believe it matters where you're buried except in the minds of the ones left behind. We're the ones who think it's nice that all the family is together in death. If I live in Sydney, I'll die there and I'll be buried there, with or without Dan. I can't imagine anyone flying my body back here. This cemetery would be closed by then anyway. Once Mum goes, I probably won't even come back myself. Things continue with the people who are living. The next baby grows up with those eyes and that hair, and somewhere down the track he or she makes the family laugh when they do something in that funny way – 'Just like Grandad.' Or Uncle, or Auntie.

A high-pitched noise makes me wince and spin around. They've begun to lower the coffin. It jerks in its sling, then stabilises, and the two assistants and Vic's sons smooth its descent into the ground. There's sobbing and Uncle Vic takes Phyll by the shoulders and pats her again and again. Father Keenan's voice continues. A trickle of sweat runs down the side of his face and his forehead is beaded with moisture. An unkind thought flashes into my mind, *If you don't stop soon you'll have to bury us all,* and I think if I'm not careful I shall turn into a sharp, outspoken village witch. Just as I reach the group, Father throws a clod of earth into the grave. It lands with a thud on the wooden lid of the coffin. Vic takes up a handful of soil and repeats the action. Then the other men follow suit and Father says the final prayer.

The crowd disperses quickly. It's too hot in the sun to hang about exchanging pleasantries and it's nearly lunchtime.

Vic walks up to Gayle and Iris. He clears his throat before he speaks. 'Phyll's prepared a bit of a spread at home, if you'd like to join us.'

Gayle turns to her mother and waits for Iris's reply.

'Thank you, Vic,' she says. 'That would be very nice.'

IRIS

Vic takes me by surprise when he comes up to us and invites us back to their place. I can't say that I've ever set foot there before. We used to meet at Mum's. It was sort of neutral territory. And later it was at the nursing home or the hospital when we were seeing to Maudie. I couldn't have expected it to be much different, not with the way things have been between Phyll and me. It's only right for a man to stand by his wife, no matter what his own opinion of the situation might be. After all, I expected Bill to take my side.

I would like to think that the invitation came from Phyll but I'm not so sure of that, although she's standing close by as he speaks and she doesn't seem to object. It's hard to tell with Phyll, what with her being so nervous all the time. You never know if it's just her general condition or if something in particular has upset her. Maybe I've been hard. I did try to fathom her from time to time but there were too many things that were just too difficult to deal with. Nell is much more tolerant but even she has had her patience stretched. Perhaps if Dad had been around for longer. Perhaps then, things might have been different for Phyll.

'Come on, Mum,' says Gayle. 'Do you want to visit Dad before we leave?'

We walk slowly over to where Bill is buried near the side fence next to a frangipani tree. I was pleased when I discovered that tree was there. I've always loved frangipanis. My plot's ready and waiting next to him. I just have to get a move on and get myself in here before they close this place down. It's only Nell that's stopping me. I can't imagine going and leaving her behind, but I would hate for her to go first. It would be so lonely without her. She's been in my life for longer than anyone else.

When I look around this cemetery, it occurs to me that I probably know more people lying in here than I do living in town. Gayle tells me not to be so silly, but it's true.

I hate funerals. They make me feel so melancholy.

Phyll has gone ahead with Vic to get things ready and the rest of the mourners have taken off, anxious to get out of the heat and find a cool drink. Gayle walks me back toward the car where Nell is waiting. Doug comes striding up, and as he puts out an arm to help guide me over a rough spot on the path, he leans forward and whispers, 'Have you been checking out your spot?'

Well, that's it for me. You can't stay miserable with that fellow about. What a difference it makes to have someone in the family who can make you laugh.

KATE

The cement is still cool from Vic's early morning hosing and the air sits light against my skin. It's such a relief to be out of the heat. I can feel the warmth evaporating into the freshness of the space and I find the old squatter's chair to stretch out in. The garden beds around the outside give the impression of walling in the space under the house. They're ablaze with crotons in splendid reds and yellows and greens, incandescent pinks and purples. Colour is what I miss most when I'm away from this place. Even the greenness of the grass rushes out to grab you by the throat and dazzle you with its vividness.

Uncle Vic sees me fingering the bright leaves. 'You won't get those down south,' he says. 'They don't like those cold winters.'

Auntie Phyll fusses about. The egg-and-bacon pie was left in the oven too long and has shrivelled on top. 'Iris always made the perfect egg-and-bacon pie!' says Phyll, 'Lucky I made meatloaf as well.'

'Don't worry, Auntie Phyll. We're hungry enough to eat the family dog, if you had one.' Phyll looks at me without smiling, then quickly rearranges slices of tomato and beetroot on a plate. I take a slice of pie and snap off the dried-out crust. The crispy lettuce from Vic's vegie garden is sliced thinly into a salad with celery and topped with a layer of cheese cubes and sliced hard-boiled eggs, and there's French onion dip with biscuits and pickles and chutney.

Auntie Iris has turned quite pink, she and Mum have laughed so much. Their eyes glisten behind their shiny specs. They lean in toward each other and laugh about things they did together and people they knew, and they keep interrupting each other to take up the story. They talk loudly for all of us to hear but the stories are really only for them. Phyll was so much younger that she can't share all of these memories. I love Auntie Iris. She smells of tea-roses and talcum powder. In her purse she carries a lace-edged hanky. Her hair is freshly permed with a lavender rinse, and her eyes weave a merry dance when she tells stories about dances and soirees and card nights and picnic days. I can see the old Iris from the days before she married Uncle Bill and, as Mum says, the change came over her. When I look at her, I see my mum. I see two young girls in crisp white cotton, arms entwined, sharing some innocent joke that I wouldn't give the time of day to, even though I would give almost anything to be able to enjoy it with someone as they do.

Uncle Vic pours me a shandy without asking. I decide not to disappoint him and take it quietly. It's not that I mind half-strength beer, but the bitterness of the hops coated with sweet lemonade is sickly. At the first opportunity I tip the drink onto a croton and pour a cup of tea instead. I can feel a headache coming on with the heat and a tropical migraine is too much to tolerate.

More people arrive, ducking beneath the decorative timberwork and into the cool space under the house. Snatches of conversation. 'Nice ceremony. Good to get it over early before the heat of the day.' 'Father Keenan. Isn't he Mary O'Dowd's grandson? You can see the resemblance.' 'Didn't her family move down to Mackay? No, I'm sure her daughter married one of the . . .' 'Last I heard they were living out Bluewater way.' 'Was that Alec Townsend from the St Vincent de Paul shop?' 'So he should. Maudie was his best customer.'

Laughter, and a pause, and the conversation changes.

I look around at the family interspersed amongst the other guests and realise that Gayle is my only close woman relative who's not geriatric, and even she is a grandmother. We are the only women left to carry on the line. Our surnames may come from our fathers but what women pass on is substance. It's in the way of doing things. Men deal in names in registers, but it's the women who preserve the family links.

It has been days since Dan and I talked properly. His message on my voicemail says, 'Ring me. I miss you.'

I miss him too and I promise myself that I'll ring him as soon as we get back to the Island. While the things happening around me haven't been earth-shattering, they have taken my attention and allowed me to avoid thinking about the fertility program. He needs to let the clinic know if we want to start again. I need to decide if I want to go ahead at all. I feel guilty at how I am making him tread water. He is so patient with me but I still need to be sure that I won't do the same things I resent my mother for doing. I need to feel certain I can be a good mother and I need to believe that Dan wants this child for more reasons than just to make me happy.

'Top-up, love? What have you done with your drink?' I think Uncle Vic has a soft spot for me. When Dad died, Uncle Vic took to doing things for Mum. Little things like picking her up at the ferry and driving her to the doctor. Helping her with her shopping, doing little chores in town so she wouldn't have to make the trip from the Island. He takes his role of the Man of the Family seriously. I hold up my teacup but he's already looking past me to Gayle. Doug is standing over her, pouring fresh drinks, being solicitous. I wonder if he wants to impress the family.

Phyll tries to be the joker of the family but she's betrayed by the shrill, nervous edge in her voice. Sometimes the effort she puts into making things light is too exhausting to keep up with. I want to get away, not think, not participate, and not follow everyone's expectations. Fall into bed and suck my cheeks in to relieve the ache of all that laughing, all that smiling. It's not good for you. Uncle Vic understands. Sometimes even he says, 'Give it a rest, Phyll.' She's always laughing, and always scratching. Hives, she calls it. She's busy making more tea and from my possie deep in the swag of the squatter's chair I watch Uncle Vic watching Doug.

I miss the point when the sharpness appears. Like the change in the conversation, the hard prattle of recriminations replaces the mellow sentiments shared just moments before. It's just suddenly there. It's crept up behind us and stolen the moment.

Someone says, 'She had a good life.' I'm tempted to throw a stone in the pond, but I've been down this road before with Mum and there's no point embarrassing her today. She steps in quickly and says, 'Maudie was well looked after,' as if that makes a good life.

'Never thought of anyone else.' Uncle Vic's voice has an edge to it that I've never heard before. Phyll says, 'That's enough, Vic.'

'Enough? There's never been enough.'

'Of course there is, Vic. We appreciate your help. We always have.' Mum's voice is soothing. It's the one she used to use to calm the hysterical tantrum I'd have just before exams.

'But you've not *given* it. Always fussing over Maudie. You never thought of Phyll. There were plenty of times with the depression when we could have done with a bit of understanding and a helping hand, but you lot have always been too concerned with what outsiders might think.'

Mum looks shocked. 'That's not fair,' she says, but the words hang in mid-air.

Gayle's grandson stops midway in clambering down from his chair. Iris reaches toward him. He slips and tumbles to the floor. The lid of his trainer cup flies off, releasing a spray of sticky red cordial. From all sides the adults leap up with cries of 'Oh no, it's over everything!' and 'Quick, rinse it out.' Phyll runs to get a damp cloth. Voices have risen on the strength of a couple of beers and a lot of emotion. Uncle Vic moves to pick up the squealing kid but Doug's rich bass tones cut in as he lifts the boy upward with a strong swing. 'We'd better get you into a bath, lad,' he says. 'You're a sticky little monster, Justin.'

Mum turns her attention to Iris's new skirt, now with a garish pink swathe across its beige pattern. 'We should rinse that out straight away.' She leads Iris off, leaving Phyll with Uncle Vic. Uncle Vic sways slightly and looks at Phyll. 'They should have been there for you, Phyll. You should have had your sisters to help.'

Phyll clasps his arm and says, 'I didn't want them, Vic.' She wraps her arms around his shoulders and squeezes him. 'Let it go, love. Let it go,' she says, and turns and walks outside. Then the moment is gone and I wonder if I've heard right.

PHYLL

Iris called her daughter Gayle and the baptism was held after Mass one Sunday in the church opposite Mum's house. Father Moran, who had married Iris and Bill, was the parish Priest and Jack and Nell were the godparents. Gayle had a christening robe that Bill's sister made out of pieces of silk left over from Iris's wedding dress and yards of Nell's hand-made lace threaded with satin ribbon. Gayle nestled like an angel on a bed of ivory. She was beautiful.

I know this because of the photo that sat on a table in Mum's sitting room.

To see her but never hold her like a daughter, never call her mine, never know the pleasures of buying her first pair of shoes, her first school uniform, seeing her grow and change, these things cut through me. In the middle of Iris's happiness, there was no mention of my sorrow because no one knew about my daughter. I wanted to call her Gay. I wanted her to have a happy life. It was the happiest name I could think of.

Iris christened her daughter Gayle.

At night I tried to stifle my misery in the pillow but it wasn't enough. Iris settled her weight onto the mattress beside me and wrapped her arms around me and said, 'I know, love. I know.' She didn't really and that was the truth of it, but with those words at least she acknowledged what I was feeling. It's the only time I've ever known Iris to be soft. Nell said nothing and Maudie didn't know. My baby lay in a small grave under the fig tree in the churchyard at Tully. Auntie Lizzie spoke with the Priest and Uncle Denny took it in and buried it at night, wrapped in the pink layette she'd made. The baby's name didn't appear in the church records but at least it lay in consecrated ground.

I watched Iris and Nell holding Gayle, stroking her face and her tiny fingers, and not a word did either of them say about my daughter. That's when I buried it all deep inside.

Vic and I met and married and I didn't even tell him. I couldn't. I didn't really understand it all myself and I still don't.

When our first son, Peter, was born in Tully, I so wanted a daughter to fill that space. I wanted it so much I had convinced myself that the baby would be a girl. Mrs Calleja kept looking at me and shaking her head at the clothes I was making in pink. 'You not have girl. Wrong shape,' she said. I didn't believe her. Peter was a beautiful baby but he was a boy.

Somehow I got it into my mind that I hadn't lost my baby. I convinced myself that Iris's baby had died and she had taken mine, that my poor bastard child was Gayle. When she was about to make her first communion, I paid Mrs Calleja for a wonderful dress like the ones she made for the local girls. I had the material sent up from Carroll's, yards and yards of spotted organza and expensive Italian lace. Vic must have had a fit when he saw the bill but he didn't say a word. He just put it all down to my illness. He's a good man, Vic, a good-hearted man when it's all boiled down.

Mrs Calleja made a dress to be proud of. The skirt stood out to here and the bodice was pin-tucked and edged with lace right up to the lace collar. It had puff sleeves and, around the waist, an organza sash that tied at the back in a bow so big it took a yard of fabric all by itself.

Vic thought visiting Mum was a good idea. He arranged for me to go down on the train with one of the company's salesmen. I took the dress out of its wrapping and proudly showed it to Mum. She must have warned Iris because when I went over there Iris was home by herself.

'Where's Gayle?' I asked.

'She wanted to go swimming with the boys.'

'Swimming?' I said. 'You let her go swimming alone?'

'She's all right, Phyll. She's seven years old and she's with her brothers.' Iris took the dress. She didn't unwrap it. She just put it on the sideboard and poured out the tea. I didn't get to see Gayle and I didn't go to the church. On Sunday morning I was on the train back to Tully. Vic was waiting for me on the station platform with Peter, awake and restless in his arms.

KATE

The eleven o'clock ferry is right on time, pulling into the breakwater terminal from its short run down from the main stop in the city. Uncle Vic dropped us off down here because he hates having to drive through the traffic in town. There are only a handful of passengers besides Mum and I boarding the ferry here. I carry Mum's canvas shopping bag on board and wait while she chats with the deckhand as he clips her ticket.

'Do you want to sit upstairs or down?' I ask her when she catches up.

She chooses the upstairs cabin. It's smaller and you get a better view of the crossing. The day is perfect, no clouds, a clear blue sky that fades into white as it nears the horizon and not a white cap to be seen on the sea.

'It might get a bit choppy once we're clear of the breakwater,' says Mum, 'but there doesn't seem to be much wind about.'

The engine starts with a roaring noise that vibrates through the whole boat and water churns out from the back of the vessel. We pull away from the mooring and set off past recreational sailing boats and fishing trawlers tied up alongside each other in the harbour.

The wharves are packed with ships waiting to be unloaded. A container swings from a giant crane that straddles one of the ships as it lifts the metal box and deposits it neatly down on the wharf. Dad's Sunday afternoon drives used to take us out there as far we could go, to the public park at the end of the breakwater from where we could look across the channel to the Island, lightly shrouded in a mist of sea spray. On a clear day Dad would point out the landmarks all the way to the Cape and he and Mum would talk about fishing spots and picnics and what might have happened to old friends they hadn't seen for years. When we reached the place where the cement walkway finished, Dad would lift me onto the top railing where I could dangle my feet over the boulders that ran into the sea. Mum would stand close to him and always they would fall silent as if they were both reading an old and shared story in the patterns of the waves that washed across the entrance.

We sail out of the harbour and into the open sea. The day is calm and the water flat and glassy, with that exquisite shade of blue turning to green that I always associate with home. It's the sort of day to sit back and let everything just glide past.

'There's something I want to clear up with you,' says Mum.

Not now, I think, reluctant to rein in my mind when it's floating blissfully between the blue and the green of the sky.

'This idea you have that Maudie didn't have much of a life. It's not true,' says Mum.

'I know she had the job at the children's home and she had her own money and stuff, but she was just a housemaid. It wasn't like she was a teacher or a doctor or something.'

Mum's voice is sharp. 'She might have been a domestic but what she did for those children at the home . . .' She stops and swallows. When she speaks again her tone is quieter. 'It was more than the people who were supposed to be responsible for their welfare.'

'Isn't that a bit far-fetched? Look, I know you feel strongly about Maudie and I'm sure she was happy but I don't think she was curing sick children.'

'I didn't say she was a miracle-worker. She was just a very kind and caring person, and if you'd listen for once you might learn something instead of trying to be such a sophisticated know-all.'

Mum clasps her handbag tightly in her lap and struggles to hold back tears. I realise that these are not the tears of sadness at Maudie dying, these are tears of frustration at not being able to reach me. I stroke her hand and mumble, 'I'm sorry,' through the lump that's threatening to choke me. She clasps my hand firmly in return and fumbles in her bag for a hanky to wipe her eyes.

'Maudie did a lot for those children. She was devoted to them, and a lot of people who thought they were better than her took advantage of that or poked fun at it, but she carried on nonetheless.'

'What sort of things did she do?'

'The children who got sent to the home, they had nothing. They'd lost their parents, their families. There was no one to take care of them in the proper sense. The home could give them a roof and a bed but not a family. Maudie used to spend every spare minute over there, playing with them and cheering them up. She even used her own money to buy storybooks and toys. If it had been anyone else they would have been put up for some award or other, but people took advantage of Maudie. They took advantage of her generosity. Don't get me wrong,' she adds hastily, 'she enjoyed what she did and she just loved those children, like you lot. She was very generous to all of you, too.'

I remember as I got older making fun of the games Maudie and I played together. She once volunteered to be a guinea pig for childish attempts at applying makeup and willingly submitted to having a clown's face painted on her. I think Nana was a bit cross because she guessed I was bored and making fun of Maudie.

'Later, it was nothing for her to walk down the street and have total strangers – grown men and women – come up to thank her for the way she'd cared about them years before when they were children in the home.'

'How did Maudie get the job?'

'A combination of things. When they were short of money for the war effort, they wanted to cancel pensions and Maudie wasn't considered disabled enough. Dr O'Donnell put her on some new medication and his wife was on the board at the children's home, so she arranged the job. Nana wasn't happy about it but under the circumstances they couldn't refuse. At least we knew Mrs O'Donnell would keep an eye on her. In the end, Maudie stayed there for thirty-eight years. I've got some clippings from the paper about her. I'll show you when we get home.'

'So those people at the funeral . . .'

'The ones down towards the back? Yes, they worked with her over the years. It was good of them to come.'

A trace of jealousy sneaks in as I think of Maudie's life being fulfilled in this unconventional way. With all her funny, blustery, eccentric ways, she belonged to us. She was our family. What Mum has told me doesn't just give her a life of her own, it gives her a life away from us, a life that was valued by strangers for being all those things that were embarrassing to us. I have always felt sad to think she didn't have children, when she did, hundreds of them. Knowing this somehow makes her less ours, less mine. It surprises me to discover how possessive I suddenly feel of her.

'Am I ever going to see you again?' At the other end of the line Dan sounds completely miserable. 'I'm sick of cooking for myself.'

'You only want me for my domestic skills.'

'Not entirely. You have a certain entertainment value.'

'Maybe I should put Mum on so you can discuss that with her.'

'Don't get uppity with me, young girl.' Dan has a gift for mimicry and even though he has only met Mum a few times, he has her way of speaking down pat. I laugh and admit to myself that I am anxious to go home. Dan's voice takes on a more serious tone. 'The clinic called. They want us to start again next week.'

'I suppose it's that time,' I say dryly.

'I didn't think you'd be keen,' he pauses. When I don't respond he fills the gap. 'You know, if you don't want to go ahead with this, it's okay by me.'

Sometimes, when the opportunity to say what you really feel opens up in front of you, the words just won't come, no matter how much you've rehearsed your opening lines. I stand there holding the receiver and desperately wish for a cordless handset so I can walk away from Mum, who is washing dishes on the other side of the kitchen divider.

'We need to talk about this,' I mumble.

'Is your mother standing next to you?' Oh Dan. Dear, dear perceptive Dan!

'Mmmm,' I answer.

'Katey, you know I'm happy to try this program, but if it doesn't work, as far as I'm concerned, I still want a life with you. Kids or no kids, you're stuck with me.'

'That's nice, but I want you to want one as much as me.'

'I do. I'm just saying it's not more important than us being together. I've watched some of those couples in the program. They lose touch with each other. Trying for the baby takes over their lives. I don't want that to happen to us. No matter what, you will always be number one.'

'Anyone would think you'd had time to think.'

'Aha! It shows.' He gives that rich, deep chuckle that

always lifts my spirits. 'Well, it was time well spent. Now, when's your flight, or do you want to walk home from the airport?'

Home. It sounds good to hear him say it.

NELL

It's that time again, that awful time when you have to wave your family goodbye and a gulf seems to open up in front of you and threatens to swallow you whole.

I wish the word goodbye didn't exist but there's no point wishing. It doesn't make the hollow, sinking feeling go away.

Kate isn't telling me everything. She doesn't realise how I can fill in the bits that are missing.

'How's Dan?' I ask when she gets off the phone.

'Okay,' she says. Nothing more, just 'Okay.'

I sense that she and Dan are settling down. I know that I can't expect her to do things the same way I did them. It's a different world but I wish she had more respect for the values we gave her, and I wish I had a way to tell her that without getting her hackles up.

Some things you just have to learn to live with.

She leans over my shoulder and looks into the pot that I'm stirring on the stove top.

'What are you making?'

'Green tomato pickles,' I say. 'Do you want the recipe?' I don't say that I've been going through my glory box, sorting out the things I want her to have. Instead I tell her, 'I came across my old recipe for rosella jam and one that Nana gave me for green tomato pickles.' I don't say that Dan might like it with leftover cold roast, the way her father did. I was going to put it into the old chest along with the other things I want her to have, thinking she'd find it in due course and use it however she wants to.

'What's green tomato pickles?' she asks.

'I only have the list of ingredients. You have to experiment with the quantity to make it work for you.'

'Why don't you come down for a visit?'

'Maybe later, when the weather warms up.'

'We might be in a new place by then.'

'Oh right,' I say, trying to sound noncommittal.

'Yeah, we're looking for a house. We'd like a bit of a garden.'

So there it is. Out in the open.

KATE

The orange tree that grows outside my mother's back door is a bush orange grown from a seed that came from the tree that stood in Nana's backyard.

'How do you know?' I ask my mother.

'She gave me some oranges and I planted the seeds.'

'And they came up there?'

'Not quite. I grew the seedlings in pots and when they were a good size I planted them out. I put some over there on the vacant allotment and the two strongest ones I planted here, on either side of the back door. Each day I watered them with the leftovers from the teapot. That kept them moist and the tealeaves must have fertilised them well because I always got a good crop of oranges.'

The one remaining tree is stumpy and marked along its thin trunk. It has survived droughts and cyclones and childish games and pets. Its leaves are a deep glossy green. Right now it is sprinkled with sweet-scented blossom and the beginnings of a new crop. In the shade about its roots I notice the fresh green of tender young leaves springing from the ground.

'Are they seedlings too?' I ask.

'The fruit never falls far from the tree,' says Mum. 'Do you want one to take back?'

'Will it grow in a pot in the flat?'

'If you keep it watered and give it some fertiliser now

and again, it'll last for a good while. You can transplant it when you move into the house.' She takes a trowel and gently lifts the largest of the plants from the soil. 'I'll wrap it in some damp paper,' she says, 'and a plastic bag so it won't dry out on the plane.'

There's a house down at the end of the bay. From the shops on the esplanade you can't make it out because of the way its weathered old wood sits nestled in the shadow of the hill, and the Norfolk Island pines stand straight in front of it, hiding it from curious sightseers. In all the years that I have been coming to the Island, I have never known any-one to live in that house. I have never seen a sign of life, no open door or light at the window.

The spot where the house sits is protected from the northerlies that blow up through the channel, sometimes at gale force. The mountain behind it throws an arm out to sea, making a headland that directs the wind around through the centre of the bay. It's one of those freaks of nature and I'm not quite sure whether it was by chance that the house was built in this protected spot, or whether some canny settler spotted the advantage of that position before choosing it as the site for his hut.

I follow the back way down to the beach to avoid having to talk to other early risers on the esplanade. This is my last morning and I want to hold each moment to myself. The back way takes me through the sandy bed of the stream that occasionally, in monsoon season, carries water down from the hills. The fine white sand is unusual in this bay, where the beach is coarse-grained granite that glows orange in the early morning sun. My feet sink into the powder between clumps of bindi-eye that tear at the trailing fringe of my towel.

I walk around past the surf lifesavers' hut and make for a thin track that leads up between the boulders. This is the way to the front door of the house, but I veer off halfway up the slope and slip between two rocks. I have to flatten myself against the smooth planes and crawl to reach the other side. Once through, I'm onto a small corner of beach hidden from the swimmers in the bay.

This corner captures the first sun before the freshness of the night leaves the air. There is a moistness here that wraps itself around the skin. I stand on the wet sand and feel the tug of the sea as it sucks the grains from under my feet with the outgoing flow of the tide. The point is behind me, so there is nothing to hold back the northerly, and even on a mild morning like this one it flies along at a pace and whips up white caps on the water.

I take a deep breath and fill my lungs with ozone, so strong it leaves me feeling heady. The sea washes around my feet and splashes up to my thighs. This is not really a beach, just an exposed corner of sand that falls quickly away to deep water. The waves smash up against the rocks with a thundering noise that drowns the sound of the seagulls and the air is laden with spray. I feel as if the sea washes my mind as clear and uncomplicated as each grain of sand.

I left my mother sleeping. She sleeps and wakes in fits and starts throughout the night, but in the early morning she falls into a deep sleep that carries her through till the ferry sounds its horn to hurry along the latecomers for the workers' boat. When I left, she was lying on her stomach, snoring into the folds of the pillow. The thought of her brings tears to my eyes. In a few hours I will be on the ferry and on my way back south. She will be alone again in her house on the Island. There will be hours of flying between us, too much for a day, a weekend, a brief visit. We may never see each other again.

When she dies, I will be the one who slips my moorings, the one who drifts away from this place. In my mind she will always be here, underscoring what I do and what I say. The decisions will be mine – the choices and directions – but she will be with me in everything that I do, not guiding, not telling, just there. It will be sad to lose her physical presence. I will miss her calls and still want her advice, but I have already slipped her out of my everyday life. My throat will tighten and I will fight back tears at small memories of her, like the brush of her dry hand against mine or, in her voice, the concern for me that no one else will ever be able to match. She is part of me. In everything I do and say, she is a part. Maybe it is the constant tugging and pushing, wanting to be part of each other, yet wanting to be separate; maybe that is what keeps us moving.

Dan, my dear, dear Dan. I think of the children we might have if we keep trying and the constant rub of their needs against mine – their wants, their ideas against mine. It no longer seems so daunting. As Mum said, you just do what you believe is right, accept the outcome, and pray for the day when it all falls into place. I've been so frightened of making mistakes that I've not made much at all. The waves washing in and out over these rocks every morning, every season, every year have worn them into the giant, smooth-edged boulders that I love. It's neither good nor bad, it just is. I can stop trying to predict the future and just live with the wash of the tide.

For the moment, the excitement of going home to where I live is tempered by the sadness of my impending departure from this place that is my heart's home. In a few hours I will take the ferry as I have on other clear mornings. The sound of the boat engines as we pull away from the jetty will be deafening and I will stand on the back deck waving at the small figure on the esplanade until it disappears from view.

And, in my memory, it will always be the same.

ACKNOWLEDGEMENTS

Many people encouraged me as a writer and assisted me in bringing this story into being. My thanks go to all of them.

This story began with my mother, Frances Donovan, who nurtured my storytelling efforts from childhood and encouraged me to believe I could do anything. Much of the historical authenticity in this novel is due to her keen memory and eye for detail and she willingly assisted me with information and advice that have enriched the fictional landscape of the story.

My great thanks go to Jennifer Smith who guided me through the major period of writing, to Professor Hilary Yerbury whose advice and encouragement helped me take my ideas into writing, and to Gaire Neave and Nicola Forbes for their generous research assistance and advice. The story also drew on a broad base of research in which I was assisted by the staff of the North Queensland Collection and the History Department at James Cook University.

So much of my growth as a writer I owe to my UTS writing colleagues Nikki Gemmell, Chris Doran, Mary Winter, Graham Williams, Stephen Muecke, Glenda Adams. I am also grateful to Fay Howard, Dawn Reed, Bev Stevenson and Denis Donovan who stepped in with valuable feedback at a crucial stage in the preparation of the manuscript.

My very special thanks go to Emelia Bresciani for her generous assistance in bringing the manuscript out of the shadows, and to my agent Selwa Anthony, and publisher Julie Gibbs, for giving this book life. I would also like to express my gratitude to all the people at Penguin Australia who have helped to bring this novel to its readers, especially Meredith Rose, Polly Croke and Melissa Fraser, who have cared for the manuscript and its fledgling author so well.

Writing is a long and often lonely occupation and to Mary Ranclaud, Dennis, Alessandra and Brendan Donovan, Kaye Weaver, Paul and Kathy Summers, Gillian Clyde, Rita Avdiev, Susan Jarvis and Virginia Melrose, thank you for your constant encouragement.

And to Michael Donovan, my loving thanks for always being there and for making it fun.